Mystery at the Rodeo

Gerald Hoff

Mystery at the Rodeo

Gerald Holt

To order additional copies of this book, contact:
Xlibris Corporation
1-888-795-4274
www.Xlibris.com
Orders@Xlibris.com
123574

Contents

CHAPTER 1	Things go Wrong	7
CHAPTER 2	Thieves Strike Fast	12
CHAPTER 3	Billy Leads the Way	17
CHAPTER 4	A Man with a Limp	21
CHAPTER 5	Thieves Strike Again!	26
CHAPTER 6	All is not Lost	30
CHAPTER 7	Wally and the Stooges	35
CHAPTER 8	Buckle Rubbings	40
CHAPTER 9	Bound and Gagged	46
CHAPTER 10	DeeDee and Fred	52
CHAPTER 11	A Clown's Face	59
CHAPTER 12	The Silver Buckle	64
CHAPTER 13	An Important Letter	69
CHAPTER 14	Front End Loader	72
CHAPTER 15	A Clown in Green	77
CHAPTER 16	Two of a Kind	81
CHAPTER 17	Billy Butts In	86
CHAPTER 18	A Grand Finale	92

Other Works by Gerald Holt

The Ghostly Tales of Mr. Tooth

Ben and Jacky and the Missing Diamond

Tails of Flame

Flames in the Ruins

The Mountain Bike Mystery

The Mystery of the Secret Caves

CHAPTER 1

Things go Wrong

THE WHITE-PAINTED HOSPITAL bed sped faster and faster down the street, swaying from side to side. It bounced and scraped along the concrete curb of the sidewalk, the thick tubular metal legs screeching in agony. Megan fought to hold on as the small wheels wobbled uncontrollably sending tingling vibrations through her hands. With a harsh metallic scraping that set her teeth on edge, the bed came to a sudden stop. It tilted forward and upwards, like a giant catapult, and Megan soared into the air.

Megan opened her mouth to scream, but then realized she'd been awakened from a bad dream by the sound of the back door slamming. Feet thudded on the wooden stairs of the old farmhouse, each heavy footstep seeming to echo round and round in her head, bouncing off the top and sides of her skull. She was wet, covered in perspiration, her long fair hair plastered to her forehead. The bed felt clammy and cold. Why couldn't Jack learn to shut doors normally like everyone else?

"Jack Perry!" Her mother's voice was raised. "You get down here right now!"

The thudding on the stairs stopped as if turned off by a switch.

"But, Mum!"

"Don't you '*but, Mum*' me, Jack. Down here now!"

"Yes, Mum." Jack's voice croaked. Megan knew he wasn't crying or anything like that, it was just that sometimes when he spoke these days, in his old high voice, his voice seemed to crack and went deeper. He couldn't control it.

Footsteps went slowly and quietly down the stairs. Megan strained to hear what was being said. She didn't want to get out of bed as she desperately wanted to get better for the parade. Why had her bed crashed? It was the first time the school had entered the bed races held the evening before the annual rodeo. Until the crash they'd been in a good position to win one of the prizes. They'd won two heats and had beaten the team from the 'Empty Hole' doughnut shop, last year's runner up. The prizes were funny. The first prize was a hospital bedpan; it was painted gold. The second prize was an old fashioned white china chamber pot with flowers painted on it. The third prize was an old fashioned stone hot-water bottle. But after this accident the principal would probably cancel further entries.

And why did she have to get concussion? It wasn't fair. Carefully she leaned out of bed, closer to the door. Her brain seemed to move inside her skull, slowly like a heavy jelly. But it wasn't as bad as last night.

"How many times have I told you?" Mum's voice was raised. "How many times, Jack?"

"I don't know, Mum. But please, I've got to get ready for the rodeo."

"So has Tony, Jack. And where is he? I arranged for both of you to be let out early."

"He's coming, Mum. I was ahead of him."

"Well then, you don't need to rush, do you? And another thing: Mr. Liang hasn't brought Samantha over yet."

Megan heard Jack groan. She didn't know whether it was because Mum was on at him, or because of Samantha. Why did Jack always pretend he didn't like her friend when she knew he did? Then, through the open window, Megan heard shouting.

"Get out!" The voice was very angry, high-pitched and shrill. "Get out!"

Oh, no! Jack must have left the gate open again and Billy had escaped. Megan wanted to cry. If Billy caused trouble then maybe none of them could help at the rodeo. It wasn't Billy's fault, he was only a goat. And Mrs. Tandy's garden was so inviting right now, full of fresh springtime growth. Megan couldn't help smiling. The first time Billy had escaped was two years ago, when she was swinging on the old farm gate at the top of the driveway. Billy saw his chance and trotted quickly out of the yard and across the road. Mrs. Tandy was in her garden preparing her vegetable patch. She was bending over. Billy walked up and gave her behind a gentle nudge. Mrs. Tandy jumped as if stuck with a needle. That frightened Billy. He snorted, put his head down and charged. Mrs. Tandy went sprawling.

That was when Jack had come running up the driveway with Tony close behind. The trouble was the boys couldn't stop laughing when they saw Mrs. Tandy's face. It had been a bad day. Billy was put on his chain in disgrace and Dad had threatened to get rid of him.

Mum's voice carried up the stairs. "Did you leave that gate open again, Jack Perry?"

"I don't know, Mum. Sometimes the catch doesn't work."

"It would if you shut it properly instead of slamming it behind you." Mum seemed to bite off each word. "Ooh! Ooh! Sometimes I could scream, Jack. Get out there, right away!"

"Yes, Mum." The back door slammed.

"Argh! That boy will be the . . ."

Megan heard the back door open again.

"Hi, Mum!"

"Tony! You're back!"

"Yes, Mum. And, wow! Was that ever lucky? I grabbed old Billy just in time. He was halfway up Mrs. Tandy's driveway."

"Well, thank goodness you got him," said Mum. "Where's Jack?"

"Shutting the gate. I put Billy on the chain, but I'll take him down to the barn and give him some food, then he won't get stubborn when Samantha and her dad arrive. How's Megan, Mum?"

"Still not a hundred percent, Tony. I really don't know if she'll be fit for the parade tomorrow."

Megan groaned. She had to be fit!

"Anyway," said Mum. "As soon as you guys have had a snack, and gone with Samantha and Mr. Liang, I'll run Megan to the doctor for a check."

"Now, don't you worry." Mum smoothed Megan's fair hair away from her eyes. "Everything will be fine."

"But Samantha has never handled Billy, Mum. And when they leave the rodeo grounds tonight he'll be by himself in a strange place."

"Don't worry so, Megan. Billy won't be all by himself. There are other animals in the petting tent. And Mrs. Freeze and that boy of hers will take over from Samantha, although there won't be much cleaning to do tonight." Mum smiled. "And you can be sure Tony will see that Billy is comfortable. You know how that old goat trusts Tony."

Mum was right. From the time Dad had brought Billy home, five years ago, he'd become attached to Tony. Tony was the only one who could ride Billy up the driveway to fetch letters from the mailbox. No one else could. Jack had given up in disgust. When he tried to ride Billy, the goat would kneel and tip him off. But since Tony had put Megan on Billy's back and led him round the barn, Billy would let her climb on his back. But he'd stand still. Without Tony, Billy wouldn't move.

"Billy will be fine," said Mum. "He knows Mrs. Freeze, and you'll be there tomorrow."

Megan nodded. Mum was right. Dr. Brunet said she'd be recovered by then. He said it was lucky she'd worn her bicycle helmet. She nodded again. Hey, wow! Her brain had stayed put and the headache was gone. She was about to nod again, to be really sure, when she heard the sound of tires crunching on the gravel of the driveway. The geese trumpeted excitedly.

"Dad's home, Mum," she said.

"Right. I'll put the kettle on and clear away my designs." Mum sighed. "I wish I had more room."

Megan smiled. Mum's papers were spread all over the old farmhouse. The dining room was *The Trevelyan Group*. This month the living room was *The Willingdon Development* and *The Martello Towers Condominiums*. Each time Mum finished an interior design project the family hoped for the space to be cleared. But then along came another assignment. They hadn't eaten in the dining room for almost five months, since Christmas. That didn't matter so much, but the television was in the living room! And Mum was gradually taking over the kitchen. Megan sighed. With Dad busy, and Mum busy, the old farm was getting untidy. For a while Dad had said he'd build Mum an office, but he always had too much to do. Then, just the other night, Mum and Dad had talked about moving to a modern house. How could they? That would be terrible! She'd lose her cozy old room with its secret cupboard in the roof. Things couldn't go that wrong, could they?

CHAPTER 2

Thieves Strike Fast

"I'M SO MAD!" Jack's voice broke from a low to a high pitch. His face turned bright red.

Megan shook her head. Why did Jack get so embarrassed? Other boys' voices broke, too. She sipped the hot chocolate Mum had made.

"Someone stole my canvas bag."

"You mean that old faded green thing, Jack?"

"Yes, Dad." Jack nodded. "Tony and I were up at the arena watching the first events of the rodeo. That clown was really funny, wasn't he, Tony? The one with the limp."

"Yes," said Tony. "I thought that big Brahma bull would get him a couple of times, but he popped into the barrel so fast, the bull didn't know where he'd gone."

Jack laughed, then turned glum again. "I put my bag beside me on the bench and the next time I looked it was gone."

"Well its not much of a loss," said Mum. "It was falling to pieces and was long past repair."

"I know, Mum." Jack shook his head slowly. "It isn't so much the bag, although it was Dad's from when he was in Africa . . ."

"Don't worry about that old bag." Dad rested a hand on Jack's shoulder.

Megan thought how alike they looked, the same wavy, almost curly, dark brown hair, and those deep brown eyes. She and Tony had straight fair hair and blue eyes like Mum.

"Nothing valuable in it, I hope," said Dad.

Jack scowled. Then his brown eyes flashed angrily and his lips formed a thin, hard line. "I really am so mad," he said between clenched teeth. "If I . . ."

Megan saw Jack's hands clench into tight fists. Jack had quite a temper at times. But why was he so upset about that old canvas bag?

"He had his CD player," said Tony, "and that new disk."

"Oh, no, Jack!" Mum shook her head, her short bobbed fair hair shining in the light from the lamp above the kitchen table. "Not the disk I like, or should I say, the one I can stand?"

Megan looked at Mum and then Jack. She hoped it wasn't the new disk. There had been a running battle between Mum and Jack about his choice in music. Jack liked everything extra-loud. It started the moment he came home from school: first the back door was slammed shut; then feet thundered up the stairs; followed by the banging of the boy's bedroom door; then the thump, thump of Jack's foot on the floor as he kept time to the music. The beat of his foot sent vibrations through the walls and ceilings. Megan usually entered the house as Mum was shouting up the stairs for Jack to turn down the volume on his small stereo. Then, a week ago, Jack had brought home a new disk. It was fairly quiet and, as Mum said, it sounded like real music.

"I hope this doesn't mean we'll have a return of that grinding, off-key beat." Mum looked at Jack. "I was just getting used to being able to work again when you were around, Jack." She smiled.

"I hope so, too," said Tony, so quietly that Megan almost didn't hear him.

Megan saw Jack's eyes flash angrily once more as he glared across the table at Tony. She knew Mum had been joking, but Jack was as sensitive about his music as he was about his voice breaking.

"It's not a joke, Mum. I saved really hard for the player. It's waterproof and everything. Now some thief has it!"

Megan nodded. It was true. Jack had saved for months. He volunteered for all the extra jobs like cleaning the barn or the chicken shed. Cleaning the chickens was the worst job. She couldn't stand the smell; it seemed to stay in her clothes and her hair. Sometimes she was sure the smell was still there even after a shower.

"The police officer we saw said he doubts Jack will ever see it again." Tony looked across at Jack. "Well, that's what he said, didn't he, Jack."

Jack nodded. Megan saw his shoulders droop and he looked at the floor.

"Drink your hot chocolate, son." Dad took his hand from Jack's shoulder. Here." He picked up the steaming mug. "I know what you mean, feeling bad about some thief having something you worked so hard for. Mum and I will have a talk about it. Maybe you should have one of those new digital players. I think they're called an iPod, or something like that."

Mum nodded. "We'll have a talk."

Jack took the mug of chocolate and cupped his hands round it. "Thanks, Dad. Thanks, Mum. Mind if I take this upstairs?"

"Go ahead." Mum smiled at Megan. "You, too, Meg. It's really late and I do want you to be fully rested for tomorrow.""

Megan sighed. "Can't I finish my drink here, Mum? I want to ask Tony how Billy settled down."

"Ah, yes." Mum nodded. "How was he, Tony?"

"Fine." Tony smiled. "There's a small pony with him and they quickly became friends. And he has lots of fresh straw for bedding. He's fine."

Megan sipped her chocolate. "That's good. Who brought the pony?" she asked.

"Friends of Mrs. Freeze. They brought him just before we left. But, talking about Jack's CD player and disks." Tony looked round the table. "The police said there'd be a lot of that over the weekend. People have their wallets and purses stolen, and cars in the parking lots are broken into even though there are security guards around. They reckon there's a gang that do it every year."

Megan saw the gleam in Tony's blue eyes. Maybe it was a gang like the one they'd helped the RCMP catch on the ferries to Victoria. "Oh no you don't, Tony." Mum glared across the table. "I can see that look. Don't you dare! Leave police business to the police."

"I wasn't thinking about getting involved, Mum. I was just telling you what the police said about a gang operating at the rodeo."

"I heard what you said, Tony." Mum looked grim. "But you always poke your nose into these things. Look at that first time, when you and Jack got involved with drug smugglers."

"We didn't exactly get involved with them, Mum."

"You know what Mum means, Tony." Dad shook his head. "I agree with Mum. It's best to stay out of these things."

"But what if we see something?" asked Megan. "We can't just ignore it. We should try to help the police, shouldn't we, Dad?"

"Helping the police and getting involved are two different things," said Dad. "You've been involved in two mysteries already. That's enough. If you do see anything, report it. Okay?"

Megan nodded and glanced over at Tony. He was nodding too, but she had a funny feeling. It was Jack who had first seen the drug smugglers. And Tony had seen the girl pickpocket. What if she saw something at the rodeo?

"I won't get involved in anything, Dad," said Tony. "I'm too involved as it is: I've got the parade tomorrow morning; then I'm cleaning out the stock pens; after that I'll be at the arena, seeing how many belt buckles I can add to my collection."

Megan knew what Tony meant. He didn't collect real buckles, only rubbings. He did have one real buckle that he'd bought two years ago, but he started making rubbings last year. He'd asked for permission to enter the riders' and competitors' section with his pad of special paper and blocks of different coloured wax. He asked competitors if they would let him make a copy of their buckle. Most riders agreed and watched as Tony put a small sheet of paper over the buckle and carefully rubbed the wax over the paper. He had some really good copies, each one carefully protected in its own plastic cover. He kept the sheets in a special binder, each with a short description of the rider, where he came from, his rodeo events, his times and what wins he'd had. Megan was thinking of starting a collection of the girls in the Ladies' Barrel race and the Grand Entry riders.

"Well, remember what Dad said, Tony. And you, Meg." Mum stood up. "Time for bed, you two."

Megan hesitated. "Dad?"

"Mum said it's time for bed, Meg." Dad yawned. "And I agree." He stretched and yawned again.

Megan had to know. "But, Dad. Are we going to the cowboy pancake breakfast?"

"Ah!" Dad looked up at the ceiling, stroking his moustache. "I don't think . . ." He looked at Mum. "I don't think we should . . ." He paused. "I really don't think we should miss that. Do you, Audrey?"

Mum smiled and shook her head. "No, Alex. We shouldn't miss that."

CHAPTER 3

Billy Leads the Way

MEGAN FELT VERY full. She wished she hadn't eaten that fourth sausage. But Samantha couldn't eat it and they were so good, especially with real Maple syrup. She looked ahead, between Billy's horns, to see how Samantha was getting on with Jack. There they were. Samantha wasn't wearing her straw Stetson, it was slung on her back. Megan hoped she wouldn't get too much sun. Everything seemed fine now, although Jack had scowled when told Samantha would be with him instead of Tony. Billy had been the culprit.

Billy had refused to move from the Petting Zoo without Tony. Then he'd refused to wear the harness for the wagon. He was fine now that Tony was leading him, but for a while Megan had wondered if they'd even be in the parade. It was fun here in the wagon, being towed by Billy. The wagon was a miniature covered wagon. The white canvas cover had 'PETTING ZOO' painted in red letters on each side. The wood of the wagon was varnished and the wheels had shiny red spokes. Megan waved to the crowd lining the street. It was a bit like being the Queen, all this waving.

Tony looked back, a broad smile on his face. He wore a black, felt Stetson. He pointed ahead. Jack was bent over an old galvanized-iron bucket beside him. He shoveled horse droppings into it. Samantha was standing back, watching. Jack stood up, holding the bucket. People in the crowd started to cheer. Jack's face was red. Megan shrugged. If only Jack didn't take things so seriously; he could raise his hat and make fun of it, that's what Tony would do. Jack hurried on to catch up with the Grand Entry riders.

Leading the Grand Entry riders was Miss Rodeo. She wore a sequined outfit that glinted in the sunlight. Samantha was running to keep up with Jack. Her bucket swung from side to side and her hat bounced on her shoulders. She fell into step beside Jack. They looked funny together. Jack was tall and lanky, like Dad. The top of Samantha's head didn't reach his shoulders even though she was only a year younger. She was twelve, like Tony, but she wasn't very tall. Even Megan was taller and she was only eleven. Megan thought Samantha was just like her mum, small and petite, with straight black hair cut just below her ears. Mrs. Liang was only five foot two, and Mr. Liang wasn't very much taller.

Megan waved as they passed another group of cheering people. But were they cheering the parade or that clown? The clown, with a large, shiny black nose was pushing his way in and out of the tightly packed throng of people. He was blowing a shiny brass horn and handing out balloons to children. They were probably cheering him. He wore bright orange pants and large, dusty brown boots. A crumpled, stained, tan felt hat topped his frizzy orange hair. Over his black and white checked shirt he wore a red vest. Bright blue suspenders held up his pants. All the colours clashed. Mum would have groaned in agony; she hated colour mixes like that. The clown scurried along the street for a short way. He was limping. Maybe this was the rodeo clown? He disappeared, pushing his way into the crowd. Megan watched the balloons bobbing along above the heads, stopping every so often.

"Okay, folks." A deep voice boomed over the speaker system. "Passing us now, drawn by Billy-the-goat, is the miniature wagon from the Petting Zoo. In the wagon is Megan Perry and leading Billy is . . . ah, that can't be right . . . it says Samantha Liang." The voice faded, and then: "You're not Samantha, are you, son?"

The crowd laughed as, Tony raised his Stetson and bowed. Slowly he straightened up, shaking his head. Tony really liked the limelight sometimes. He pointed dramatically to where Samantha was now dancing around hitting the side of her galvanized bucket with the flat of her shovel. The metal against metal rang loudly in the morning air. Megan smiled. She was glad it had turned out such a sunny day; her friend was really enjoying the parade. Then she saw Jack lift his bucket to join in. As he did so it tipped, and the crowd roared with laughter as droppings tumbled to the ground. Poor old Jack, he'd tried to be funny. Now his face was red as he bent down once more to scoop it up. This time Samantha was helping.

Tony shouted something but Megan couldn't hear what he said as, behind her, the band started to play and the skirl of bagpipes drowned out Tony's voice. It was getting hot and she was glad the wagon had a canvas cover. Megan took off her jacket and stuffed it down behind her, next to the bags and her straw Stetson. All the bags were there, hers, Tony's, Jack's and Samantha's. After last night no one wanted to leave the bags unattended. Jack's was his new one, the black nylon bag he kept his soccer referee gear in.

Megan looked back at the pipers. Some were young but most were older, including one lady. They marched along proudly, their red tartan kilts swaying. Megan felt her feet moving. She'd taken Highland dancing for several years and had won a lot of medals.

The parade rounded the corner at the end of the main street. They were back at the marshalling area. The parade was over. The square was filling fast. There was the Post Express Company mail stagecoach near a group of antique farm tractors. The canvas-covered chuck wagon, drawn by a team of jet-black horses pulled in next to Ronald McDonald who was still seated in an antique open car. Next to him on the other side was Sir Ima Beaver in the Fire safety house. Jack and Samantha were over by a very old, red painted fire truck. The driver had a large, black, handlebar moustache. Samantha was smiling and chatting, but Jack had that glum look on his face.

"We have to hurry, Meg," said Tony, leading Billy and pushing his way through. "I want to be in time for the opening of the Show Tent."

Megan knew why Tony was so eager, he wanted to see the special belt buckle collection. But first they had to get Billy to the Petting Zoo tent and put the wagon in Mr. Liang's truck.

"Look," said Tony. "It will be much quicker if Jack and I unhitch Billy over there, take him to the tent and give him a feed. You and Sam take the wagon to her dad's truck. Okay?"

Megan nodded and climbed out of the wagon. It was a good idea and would save time. "Okay, Tony." She cupped her hands to her mouth. "Jack! Sam! Follow us!"

Samantha came running over. "Jack has to empty the buckets." She was grinning, tiny lines forming at the corners of her almond-shaped eyes. "I don't think he's too happy. And he has to take a full wheelbarrow-load to some place behind the old barns."

Tony laughed "Poor old Jack." He scratched Billy's head between the horns. Billy lifted his head and pulled back his lips as if smiling. "Thank you Billy, you saved me a rotten job."

Megan shrugged. "It's only horse-droppings."

Tony smiled. "I know, but you know Jack. I'll meet you guys outside the Show Tent, okay."

Megan nodded. "Do you want to take Jack's bag or should we keep them all till we meet?"

"You keep them." Tony looked at his watch. "See you in half an hour, at twelve-thirty. I'll tell Jack." He turned. "Come on, Billy."

CHAPTER 4

A Man with a Limp

"WHAT'S THAT MAN doing?" said Samantha.

"What man?" Megan looked round. She couldn't see anyone.

"Over there, by the Show Tent. See him?"

The two girls were standing beneath an old cottonwood tree at the rear of the tent. The bright midday sun cast a dark shadow round them, a shadow rippling at the edges from the slight but cooling breeze disturbing the leaves of the tree.

Sam was now pointing. Megan turned. "I see him now," she said.

The man had pushed himself up from the ground and was now hurriedly brushing himself down. He looked round quickly but seemed not to notice the girls. He started to walk away.

Samantha was whispering. "He rolled out from under the side of the tent."

"Hm! That is strange," said Megan. "Maybe he wanted to see the exhibit without paying, before it opens." She knew there were two security guards at the front entrance, and there was a ticket booth, too. She wondered if they realized how easy it was to get inside under the side flaps?

Samantha was pointing again. "Look!" she said.

The man had stopped walking and made as if to turn round. Limping towards him was another man, a brass horn hanging from a cord round his neck. He put the horn to his lips and blew a short, sharp blast. He gestured angrily, making motions with his fingers and hands. The other man did the same, walking to meet him. They stood together in an area of bare, dry, dusty ground.

For a moment Megan was confused. Then she realized what was happening. "They're talking sign language," she whispered.

"They look angry," Samantha whispered back. "I wonder what they're saying?"

Megan shook her head. "I wish I knew. Uh, oh! Now they're really angry."

The man who had rolled out from the tent was pushing and poking at the man with the horn. He backed up. The first man leaned forward; as he did so Megan saw something shiny drop from inside his coat. It fell to the ground making a small cloud of dust. Then the man with the limp turned and, with a long, loping stride started to run towards a group of horse trailers. The other man followed. They disappeared through a narrow gap between two trailers just as a security guard, wearing a pale blue shirt, dark blue pants and heavy black boots, appeared from the front of the Show Tent. He was speaking into a walky-talky radio.

Megan was about to run forward to see what the man had dropped when the brass band from the Legion marched up and halted right over the spot.

"Oh, heck!" Megan shook her head.

"What's up?" said Samantha.

"Didn't you see that shiny thing drop from his pocket?"

"Whose pocket?" Samantha's short, bobbed hair shone in the sunlight as she shook her head.

"The man who came out from the tent. It fell from his pocket onto the ground."

"Well, let's look for it."

"That's just it." Megan felt really frustrated. "We can't, not now. The band is standing right over the spot. And look at the crowd!"

The band major raised his right hand and the musicians raised their instruments. Now the band major was looking to his left. Megan saw a small group of people approaching. One wore a black and red gown. He had a shiny gold chain round his neck. It was the mayor. The band started to play and the crowd surged forward. Megan lost sight of the small group of dignitaries as people pushed in front of her and Samantha. She felt someone pull on her sleeve. She turned. It was Jack.

"Tony will be here in a minute," said Jack. "He's picking up your special pass."

That was right. Megan had forgotten. As she was helping at the rodeo, working in the Petting Zoo, she had a pass to get into all the events.

"Here he is now," said Jack.

Tony was near the band, looking round, his right hand shielding his eyes. Megan took off her Stetson and waved it. There, he'd seen them. Tony hurried over as the band stopped playing.

"Here you are, Meg. You wouldn't have been able to get into the Show Tent or the rodeo events without this."

"Thanks, Tony." Megan looked at the orange, cardboard pass. String was threaded through two holes at the top. At the bottom, in bold letters, were the words: *PASS MUST BE WORN AT ALL TIMES.* She looked at the others. No one wore a pass. "Where are your passes?"

"You don't wear it all the time," said Jack. "Hang it round your neck when you want to go into an event. If you wear it all the time people keep stopping you to ask questions."

"Oh." Megan nodded. She tucked the pass into the rear pocket of her jeans.

"Don't put it there," said Tony. "That's the first place a pickpocket will go for. Put it in your shirt pocket."

That was a good idea. Megan hadn't thought about pickpockets since the conversation at home last night. She unbuttoned the pocket of her red and white checked shirt and slipped the pass in and buttoned the flap shut. There, it was safe.

The mayor was just finishing his speech. "And I'm pleased that we are one of the first cities to be able to host this wonderful exhibition of rodeo memorabilia and cowboy fame. So, without further ado, I declare this exhibit open!"

People clapped and the crowd surged forward. The band started to play once more. This time they played, *Home on the Range*. The tune didn't sound right played by a brass band. Megan sighed. The band major smiled and threw his baton into the air and caught it, spinning it round. He lifted it high and then brought it down sharply. The band moved off at a quick march.

"Come on," said Tony. "If we don't hurry we'll have to queue to get in."

"I'm not going in now," said Megan. "It's too crowded and I'm too hot. Anyway, Sam and I have to be on duty at the Petting Zoo in a while." This was true but she also wanted to search the ground where the band had stood.

Samantha looked at Megan questioningly and then shrugged. "Go ahead, you guys," she said. "I know you want to see the buckle exhibit, Tony."

Tony nodded. "And I'm going to see if I can get permission to take rubbings." He grinned. "That would be a great addition to my collection."

"We'll see you two later," said Jack, "at the arena, for the third rodeo event. Come on, Tony."

Megan nodded absentmindedly. She was watching the band, trying to remember the spot. "See you," she said to the boys. "Come on, Sam." She hurried over to the area of dry, dusty ground. What if someone else found it?

It wasn't hard to find. They scuffed the ground with their feet and there it was.

"Look!" said Sam, excitedly.

Half-covered in yellow-brown dust and dried bark chips was what looked like a silver buckle. Megan picked it up. It was heavy, and a lot larger than the one Tony had. In the centre was the figure of a rider on a bronco. It looked old and Megan couldn't make out the lettering round the edge; it was blurred from polishing over the years.

"This is what dropped. I'm sure."

As she said this, Megan had a scary feeling, a feeling she was being watched. She looked round. By the horse trailers stood a clown in a red and white polka-dot shirt, red pants and a white cone-shaped hat with a red pom-pom on the tip. He was staring directly at them. He didn't look funny, even though he had a wide, red, lop-sided grinning mouth painted on his face and a large, round red nose. Megan shivered in spite of the hot sun. She looked towards the Show Tent. The boys weren't in sight, they must be inside. The crowd was huge and she couldn't see either of the security guards. The clown stared, unblinking, one huge, black-booted foot tapping the ground. Megan stuffed the buckle deep in her bag.

"Come on!" She grabbed Samantha's hand.

Samantha looked at her with a questioning look, her right eyebrow raised.

CHAPTER 5

Thieves Strike Again!

"WHAT'S THE PROBLEM? What's the rush?" asked Samantha.

Megan hurried along, half running through the Midway. The crowd was thick here, people moving slowly, stopping at the games' booths, or the food, ice cream and candy floss stands. The air was heavy and rich with the smells of hamburgers and hotdogs, fried onions and perogies, corn dogs, fish and chips, barbecue sauce and fried chicken, all mingled with the sweet smell of homemade fudge.

Megan glanced back over her shoulder several times. There was the clown, not far behind, pushing his way through a mass of people outside the Blue Lion Tattoo Parlour. Some people tried to joke with him but he pushed them aside.

"There's a clown following us," said Megan.

"A clown!" Samantha laughed. "Why would a clown follow us?"

"I don't know," said Megan. "But he was watching us at the Show Tent when we found the buckle. Now he's behind us."

"Why don't we ask him why he's following us?" said Samantha. "Maybe he isn't. Maybe he's just going this way too."

"I just have a funny feeling about him." Megan shivered. "Well, not funny, but scary, frightening."

Samantha shrugged. "With all the people here, Meg, he can't do anything."

That was true. Megan looked round. There were hundreds of people. The place was teaming with people. From the Midway, behind rows of booths, music blared, old and new tunes competing with each other. Mum would hate it. The Ferris wheel turned. There were screams from riders on the Quasar, the Big Dipper, and the Gravitron. The loudest screams came from the House of Horrors. Megan slowed down. They were passing a booth where a man wearing a yellow, green and blue fluorescent vest shouted above the noise around him. He was looking directly at Samantha from under a straw Stetson spray-painted in the same colours as his waistcoat.

"How about you, love?" He held three brightly coloured plastic rings. "Fifty cents a go. You'd like to win a big, cuddly toy, wouldn't you?" He looked away as Samantha shook her head. "How about you, dearie?" He held out the rings to Megan.

"No thanks." Megan turned to Samantha. "You could be right, Sam." She looked back. The clown had stopped. He was staring over his big red nose, looking at her through the crowd. "We'll ask him what he wants. Maybe he knows something about the buckle. Come on!" She started back.

"He's turned round," said Samantha.

It was true. Megan saw the clown, his back towards them, returning the way they'd come. He looked back and headed between two canvas booths. *RIFLE RANGE* said a sign over the nearest booth.

"Three shots a dollar!" shouted a woman at the booth. "Hit a duck and win a lovely prize." Rows of brightly painted ducks moved left to right across a painted pond. "Only a dollar! Win a prize!"

The clown was peering round the side of the booth. Megan started forward and he disappeared. She was about to follow, between the tents, when she stopped suddenly. Samantha bumped into her.

"Now what?" said Samantha.

"If we follow him we'll be away from the crowd." Megan shook her head. "I think he wants us to follow. Back there it's just trailers and parking, hardly any people."

"You really are scared, aren't you?"

Megan nodded. There was no sign of the clown; he could be behind either booth. Some sixth sense told her there was danger. "Come on!" She grabbed her friend's hand. "Before he realizes we aren't following him." Megan pulled Samantha along as she forced her way back.

A short time later they were at the Petting Zoo. Megan looked back before they entered. There was no sign of the clown. Good. But just in case, as soon as they were safely inside, she took the buckle out of her bag and stuffed it deep down in the pocket of her jeans. Again she looked back, peering out of the tent. No sign of the clown. "Phew!"

"Why did you do that?" said Samantha.

"Just a feeling," said Megan. "A creepy feeling. I think he saw me put the buckle in my bag."

Samantha shrugged. "I must admit, that when he turned round when we started to follow him, it was a bit odd that he ran off. But I still think you're too suspicious, Meg. Like your Mum says, you and the boys see mysteries where there's no mystery."

Megan looked at her friend. It was true. Mum did say that, and she'd said not to get involved. She looked at her watch – five minutes to two – almost time for their shift. They couldn't leave now, but after they'd done their two hours perhaps she should go to the RCMP tent and tell them what had happened.

One of the other girls helping with the animals came up. "Are you two ready to take over?"

"I have to hang my things up," said Samantha."

"Me too," said Megan. "How is Billy enjoying all this attention?"

The girl grinned. "He loves it. We tell the kids to scratch his head like you said. He stands there smiling, or at least it looks like smiling."

Megan laughed. "He can take that all day, silly old goat. I'll hang up my jacket and bag, then you can go, Tara."

"Great! See you at four." The girl turned and called across the tent. "Meg and Sam are here, Jackie. Let's go!"

Half an hour later Megan was showing a small boy how to pet the rabbits. "Gently," she said. "If you pull his ear he'll go into his house." She turned. There was noise and scuffling outside the tent. A group of about ten or twelve kids, aged between twelve and fourteen, pushed their way into the tent. They were laughing and joking, pushing each other and not caring who they bumped into. Two of the older ones were girls.

"Ooh! Look at all the lovely animals," said one of the girls.

The group moved through the tent, spreading out as they went, shouting over the heads of the children. One of the parents suggested they leave. Megan wished they would. Then one of the boys opened the gate to Billy's pen. He jumped up and down and shouted at Billy. Megan was mad. Billy had his head down to charge.

"Stop that!" Megan grabbed Billy's collar and held on tightly. "All right, Billy," she said.

The youth grinned. Megan could see that although he was short he was older, a teenager, one of the leaders. He looked across the tent, almost as if questioningly. Then he nodded, signaling with a wave of his right arm. "Okay, let's go! We'll leave these little babies to their fun." He leaned forward, his hands held on either side of his face like antlers and shouted at Billy. "Bah!" He turned and ran.

The rest of the group followed. They hadn't been in the tent more than a minute, but young children were crying and angry parents were complaining while they tried to comfort them.

Megan was finally getting Billy settled as Samantha came over. "What was that about?"

Megan shook her head. "I don't know." She looked round the tent. "But they've succeeded in spoiling a nice visit for these kids." Then, instinctively, she glanced towards the back of the tent. "Did you move my bag, Sam?"

Samantha shook her head, her short black hair waving from side to side. "No, Meg. Why?"

"It's gone," said Megan. "That's what that was about. My bag." She felt in her pocket. The buckle was still there. Thank goodness she'd moved it.

CHAPTER 6

All is not Lost

"WHAT DO YOU mean?" said Samantha a short while later.

"They were after my bag. Don't you see? It's so obvious when you think about it."

"Well, they didn't take it."

"No, they didn't. But they emptied everything out."

"Mine too." Samantha nodded. "I bet they were after money. Maybe they were looking for CD players, like Jack's."

Megan didn't think Sam was right. She was mad. They'd found their bags on the ground at the back of the tent. Hers had been turned inside out and the lining ripped open.

"Lucky I carry my change purse in my pocket," said Samantha. She was searching through the items scattered on the dirt floor. "Nothing missing as far as I can see."

"Nothing from my bag either," said Megan. She pushed the bag right side out. "But they weren't looking for money or anything like that. They were looking for the buckle."

"You can't be serious." Samantha was shaking her head. "Now I know your mum is right. You and Tony and Jack have mysteries on the brain."

Megan picked up the plastic container with her sandwiches inside. After the pancake breakfast she hadn't felt hungry at lunchtime. Now she did and also wanted a drink. Good. There was the juice. She took a sip. The apple juice was warm but wet. She started to think and remembered her thought of last night. Had it really happened? First there was Jack and the smugglers, then Tony and the pickpockets. And now her: Three mysteries! There really was something strange about the buckle, she knew it.

"You're quiet," said Samantha.

Megan nodded. She wanted to think this through. They'd have to report what had happened to the police at the RCMP booth in the Safety Fair. She looked at her watch, almost three o'clock. They were off at four, but were meeting the boys at the Stetson Bowl arena for the rodeo events. The rodeo started at four sharp and she didn't want to miss that. She hoped Tara and Jackie would be early like she and Samantha had been.

"When we get off we'll report this to the RCMP."

"Why?" said Samantha. "Nothing's missing and even if the police did find those guys, or even one of them, they'd just say the bags must have been knocked down, or something like that."

Megan knew Sam was right. What could the police do? "We can show them the buckle," she said. "The man who lost it may have reported it, and we can tell them about the clown."

"Well there isn't any rush," said Samantha. "If we do all that when we get off at four we'll miss the rodeo events. Can't we do it afterwards? I haven't seen a rodeo before."

It was true. Sam and her family hadn't been in Canada long; they'd come from South Africa not quite two years ago. And Sam was living on Galiano Island and didn't get to many events like the rodeo. It was lucky that Mr. Liang was working in Vancouver on a special project at the Vancouver Aquarium, and Mrs. Liang and Sam were here for the May long weekend.

"Okay," said Megan, hanging her bag back on the hook. She shivered. She had that funny feeling again. Was someone watching them? She whirled round just in time to see the clown dodge quickly back behind the canvas flap at the entrance to the tent. Now she knew she was right!

"Why did you turn round like that?" said Sam, hanging her bag next to Megan's.

"He was there," said Megan. "At the entrance."

"Do you mean the clown?"

Megan nodded. "And when I spun round he hid behind the tent flap."

"Wow! Maybe you're right, Meg." Samantha's right eyebrow was raised questioningly.

Megan's blue eyes were serious beneath her fair hair. "I know I'm right, Sam. And I'm going to find out about this." She thrust her hand into her pocket and ran her fingers over the outline of the silver buckle.

"Maybe we should go to the police straight away," said Samantha. "As soon as we finish here."

Megan nodded. "I don't want to miss any rodeo events but this is getting really weird."

An hour later, as the two girls left the Petting Zoo, Megan looked around. There was no sign of the clown or the rowdies who'd come into the tent. The Safety Fair wasn't far and telling their story shouldn't take long.

"Hey! Look over there!"

Megan looked where Sam pointed. There were four really old fire trucks parked side by side. In front of each bright red truck was a sign: *1912 VFD Truck; 1920 LaFrance Pumper; 1929 NWFD Mack Pumper; 1928 HUB Fire Engine.* They were beautifully polished and a man was busy rubbing the brass headlight of one of the pumper-trucks. Next to the trucks was *The Fire Safety House* with Sir Ima Beaver entertaining a group of children. But what Sam pointed at was *The DUNK Truck.* Just as Megan noticed it someone hit the centre of the target. Wham! With a shout, a man, seated in a chair above the transparent dunk tank, fell into the water. The crowd clapped and roared with laughter. Megan joined in.

The man clambered out of the tank, water streaming down his face. He pushed back his hair and, raising his fist in mock anger, grinned and sat once more on the chair.

"Not you again!" he shouted.

But almost before he'd finished, the teenage girl who'd thrown the last ball took aim and hurled another one. It just missed the target and hit the canvas screen with a resounding thunk. The crowd seemed to sigh together. The girl took aim. A third ball sped through the air. Clang!

This time the man held his nose as he was tipped into the water. The crowd roared.

"You wouldn't get me letting people do that," said Samantha. "No way." She stood watching.

"Me neither," said Megan. "But we can't stop, Sam. Come on, the RCMP stand is over there." She hurried to where a large crowd was gathered. The RCMP *Safety Bear* was shaking hands with children. Boy! It must be really hot in that outfit.

A video was playing on a large screen. "Don't talk to strangers," said a voice from the machine. On the screen a man approached some children who were playing on swings. "I've lost my little dog," he said. "Can you help me find him? He'll be so scared all by himself." One of the children got off the swing he was playing on. "NO!" boomed the voice from the machine. "STAY TOGETHER. Do not be taken in by this man's story. Ah, ha! Here comes a parent. Will the stranger ask for help to find the dog he says is lost? No! See how quickly he's moving away."

Samantha was tugging at Megan's sleeve. "We'll be late for the rodeo show."

"Right." Megan nodded. They had to speak to someone, but she couldn't see a police officer. She went to one of the tables. A community volunteer was showing an elderly lady a door lock display. "This is the deadbolt lock I was mentioning."

"Excuse me," said Megan.

The elderly lady looked at her angrily.

"I won't be long," said the volunteer. He took a brochure from the table. "This describes the various locks and how they should be fitted."

Megan looked round. Maybe there was a police officer in the small tent behind the display tables. She walked towards it.

"Hey!" The volunteer stood up. "Where do you think you're going?"

"I wanted to see if there's a police officer here. I want to report something."

"Is it an emergency?" asked the man.

Megan shrugged. "Well, not really, I guess. But my bag and my friend's bag . . ."

The man didn't let Megan finish. "Stolen?" he asked.

"No, but we . . ."

"Well, you'll have to wait till I'm finished here. The duty officer is attending to a theft from auto." The man turned back to the lady.

"Young people these days," said the woman. She glared at Megan.

Megan was upset. They'd come to report something the police could be interested in. She turned to Samantha. "Let's come back after the rodeo show," she said. "It may be less busy then."

"And there might be a real police officer," said Samantha, loudly.

Megan saw the volunteer look at Sam angrily. The lady was glaring, too. "Kids these days!"

"Come on!" said Samantha. "And don't forget to wear your pass." She started to run. "We'll be late."

"Coming!" Megan took the bright orange pass from her pocket and hung it round her neck.

CHAPTER 7

Wally and the Stooges

"HI, JACK."
"Oh, hi, Samantha." Jack
moved his black bag from the wooden bench beside him. "You guys
are late. They've already had the bareback bronco and the saddle
bronco events."

"What's on now?" said Megan, making herself comfortable on
the bench. She hoped they hadn't missed the bull riding. She pulled
her Stetson down and forward, shielding her eyes from the sun. It was
getting quite low now.

"Steer wrestling," said Jack. "But it's almost over. Hey! Look at
that guy!"

The rider had been waiting behind a rope barrier to give the steer
a head start, but with a shout of 'yee-ha!' he was out of the chute
urging his horse forward. He drew level with the steer and as the
horse surged forward the rider leapt from the saddle, legs extended.
He grabbed the steer's horns. It was over in seconds. In a single move
he brought the steer round in a tight arc and then, placing his left
hand under the animal's jaw, caught it off balance and threw it to the

ground. It lay flat on its back, all four legs extended. The rider stood up and brushed himself off. He was a big, powerful man, well over six feet tall. The steer scrambled to its feet and trotted off to the side.

"Wow! That was fast," said Jack.

The loudspeakers crackled and a voice boomed out over the ring. "What did I tell you, folks? At six foot six and two hundred and thirty pounds, they don't make skates big enough for Shorty Steve Sanders from Smithers, so he gave up hockey for the rodeo."

The crowd laughed and the rider doffed his hat, running his fingers through unruly, straw-coloured hair.

The speakers crackled again. "Time to beat was four point two seconds. Shorty's time is three point eight! Now that's *really* hard to beat."

Megan cheered, but she felt sorry for the next cowboy, waiting his turn across the arena.

"Wow!" Jack looked at his program. "I bet he wins. Only two more riders, then its calf roping."

"When do they have the bulls, Jack?" asked Samantha.

"After the calf roping," said Jack.

Megan could hardly wait. The bull riding was her favourite event. The bulls weighed from fifteen hundred pounds to two thousand pounds, and the riders had to stay on them for eight seconds.

Soon the calf roping was over and the arena became hushed.

A clown came out in a bright green, padded barrel, pulled by a rooster strutting along with a small harness over its neck and body.

The voice boomed over the speakers: "I can't believe it, folks. Is that a grown man out there?"

The crowd laughed.

The clown stopped and stared at the media booth and then round the arena. He let go the reins and motioned with his hands.

The speakers crackled. "What's that, Wally. Oh, I'm sorry. I didn't mean to hurt your feelings." The voice boomed out again. "What's that? Oh, I see. You want two pickup men?"

The clown nodded.

"Why do you want the pickup men, Wally?"

The clown signaled again with his hands and fingers. Megan nudged Samantha.

"That's one of them," she said. "The men we saw outside the Show Tent."

"Shush!" Jack glared at her, his dark eyebrows low over his eyes. "I can't hear."

The voice was continuing. "You want the pickup men to pick up the droppings?"

The clown nodded again and pointed round the arena.

"Wally,' said the announcer. "Pickup men don't pick up droppings. Pickup men help riders in the arena, getting them out of the way of the bulls and broncos. You should know that by now."

The clown signaled again.

"Okay, Wally, we'll send someone out."

A door opened beneath the media booth and two clowns shuffled out. One was tall and thin the other one short and fat. Both wore red and white striped pantyhose under bright purple shorts. They had green and yellow striped shirts, and the tall one wore a ten-gallon hat that made him look even longer and skinnier. The short one wore a flat cap. They both carried a shovel in one hand, and between them they carried a shiny, galvanized metal garbage can. They put it down and started to talk.

Megan saw Wally-the-clown reach down into his barrel. He pulled out a brass horn and blew two very loud short blasts. The other clowns jumped, looked round and then continued talking.

"It is him," said Megan. "The one with the horn."

"Shush!" Jack looked at Megan again. "Quiet, Meg! Watch!"

Megan was annoyed that no one was listening to her, not even Sam. Wally-the-clown was one of the men they'd seen arguing outside the Show Tent.

Wally reached into the barrel again. He looked round the arena, smiling, holding up the biggest firecracker Megan had ever seen.

The crowd laughed and the other clowns looked round. Quickly, Wally hid the firecracker, stopped smiling and shrugged. The clowns started to talk again.

Wally lifted the firecracker slowly and held it to the side, away from him. Then he reached into the barrel and brought out an enormous match. It was alight. Again the crowd laughed.

The two clowns looked round again, but Wally had put the firecracker and the lighted match into the barrel. The crowd gasped.

"He'll blow himself up!" said Jack.

Megan could hardly believe it. What was Wally doing? The firecracker would explode if the match caught the fuse.

The two lazy clowns turned away. Wally pulled out the match and the firecracker. The fuse of the firecracker was spluttering and almost burnt down. With a flourish, a wink and a smile, Wally leant forward and tossed the firecracker and match into the garbage can. There was a loud clunk.

Megan held her breath.

The other two clowns glanced over, shrugged and turned back just as there was an enormous booming explosion. Smoke billowed from the can as the clowns fell flat on their faces.

"Oh, no!" Wailed the voice over the speakers. "What have you done now, Wally?"

Wally tugged on the reins and he and the barrel moved forward, the rooster crowing and flapping its wings.

Megan could now see that the rooster wasn't actually pulling the barrel. The barrel didn't have a bottom and she could see Wally's dusty, brown leather boots and the legs of a pair of orange pants.

Wally stopped by the two clowns. He winked and reached into his barrel again. Out came a bucket. Wally tilted it over the thin man, pouring a stream of water over his head. With a yell, the man jumped up just as Wally poured the rest of the water over the fat man. The fat man yelled and rolled to the side knocking over his friend who fell headfirst into the smoking garbage can.

The crowd was roaring with laughter. Wally reached into his barrel again and brought out a whip that he cracked over his head. Then he leaned back, tilting the barrel so that the rooster's feet were just off the ground and ran, limping, out of the arena. He blew a raspberry on his horn as the fat man pulled his friend out of the garbage can. The thin man, his face black, shook his fist. And shouting loudly the two clowns chased after Wally.

"Thank you, Wally and the Stooges!" Boomed the voice over the speakers. "You know, folks, Wally once told me he was a bull rider, but he had to stop riding bulls on doctor's orders. Seems he had a stomach problem." There was a pause. "Do you want to know what the problem was, folks?"

The crowd roared.

"Yes!" shouted Jack, his voice breaking from a low to high pitch.

Megan looked at her brother. He was enjoying himself so much that he hadn't noticed his voice break.

"Well, folks. The problem was . . . NO GUTS!"

Megan shook her head as the crowd groaned.

A man next to her laughed. "What a corny one," he said. "That really is an old joke."

CHAPTER 8

Buckle Rubbings

"NOW FOR THE bulls," said Jack. "See, they're getting ready over there."

Megan watched the men in the chutes beside the media tower. Cowboys straddled the thick tubular metal fencing. The riders stood by inspecting their rigging.

"Where's Tony?" asked Samantha.

Megan had wondered that, too.

Jack pointed to the section beside the chutes, on the far side of the media tower. "Somewhere in there, taking rubbings and talking to the cowboys."

"Again?" said Samantha. "He collected buckle rubbings all day yesterday – well, not *all* day, not when he was working."

"I know." Jack nodded. "But he's getting a really good collection. He got Old Wally's buckle last night."

"Wally's!" said Megan. "He didn't tell me."

"Or me," said Samantha.

"Can we go over there?" said Megan. She wanted to show Tony the buckle in her pocket. She could feel it through her jeans. It almost seemed hot in her pocket, pressing against her leg.

Jack shook his head. "Tony has special permission. But you can see him if you climb up there at the end of the stands. You can look down into the waiting area where the riders get ready."

Megan didn't want to do that right now. The bull riding was about to start. "I'll wait till after the bull riding." She'd forgotten about the clown until Jack mentioned Tony's buckle collection, but there was Wally once more in the arena. He didn't have his rooster with him this time. He limped along, rolling a very large, orange and blue, padded barrel to the centre of the arena. He waved and the crowd cheered.

"I heard you talking about Old Wally Deeze," said a man behind Jack. "He's been a fixture on the rodeo circuit for years, ever since his accident."

"His accident?" Megan turned round. "Is that why he can't talk?"

The man shook his head and removed his old brown felt Stetson. He ran his fingers through thin, graying hair. The hat had made a red line across his forehead. "Nope." He replaced the hat and settled it back down on his head. "He was born like that, but it's the reason why he limps."

"Oh!" Megan was interested. "What happened?"

"Used to be a bull rider some twenty years back," said the man. "He'd come off many a bull in his time; broken ribs, arms, broke his jaw once. He was laid up for almost a year, had it wired up."

"And he came *back*?" Megan couldn't believe it.

"Yep." The man smiled. "Rodeo's in his blood. He was back a couple of years when a big Brahma stomped on his leg. It trampled him real good. He couldn't ride the bulls no more, so he's out there clowning and helping make sure others don't get hurt like he did. Not like that brother of his."

"What does his brother do?" said Jack.

"It's not what he does." The man paused, shook his head and continued. "It's what he used to do." He looked over Megan's head. "Uh, oh! That didn't last long."

While they were talking the first rider had come out. He was a youngster and was now walking slowly back to the gate, holding his back. The crowd laughed, as Wally, limping along, just ahead and just out of reach of the bull, made the huge animal turn in tight circles. Then he tripped. Snorting, the bull charged. Wally only just had time to leap into the barrel as the fat clown with the striped stockings distracted the animal. The bull looked round and then back to the spot where Wally had been. Wally popped his head out of the barrel and gave a blast on his horn. The bull turned, snorting and pawing the ground.

"Old Wally's been a bit off today," said the man. "That's the third mistake he's made. Not like him."

The bull was now chasing the thin clown and was soon in the corral.

"No score for the last rider," a new voice boomed out of the speaker. "But not to worry, that 'ornery old bull has thrown many a rider. Now, here comes Rocky Peters on Devil's Fire."

The chute gate opened and a black bull charged out with a rolling, twisting motion. It was small but powerful and Megan could see muscles rippling beneath the shiny black hide. It twisted and bucked, reversing in a lurching spinning effort to get the rider off its back. The cowboy's leather-gloved hand gripped the rope tied round the bull, just behind the shoulders where a heavy metal bell hung down clanging to annoy the animal.

"This fella can sure ride," said the man behind Megan. "Look at the way he sits forward and uses his free arm."

Megan watched. The cowboy was using his arm and body to counter the bull's spins and lunges. It kicked hard, its hooves hitting the ground sending up clods of mud mixed with sawdust and shredded bark. How could the rider stay on? Then a buzzer sounded. The eight seconds were up.

The cowboy released his grip, slid off the bull's back and ran for the fence. The bull charged after him, a seething black mass. But, just before it reached the running man, Wally came into view, sounding his horn. The bull came to a sudden halt, turning to face this new problem. The cowboy leapt for the fence and jumped down on the far side.

Down went the bull's head. It charged. But Wally was in the barrel quick as a flash this time.

"A fine ride by a fine competitor," boomed the voice over the speakers. "An eighty-two! That'll be a hard one to beat. Rocky Peters, folks. Eighty two."

"Hey! Look at these!"

Megan turned. There was Tony, scrambling up through the stands waving a handful of paper.

"I got Ray Tompkins, Jim Mahoney and Pete Hayes. And look at this one. He's Australian."

"Australian?" said Samantha.

Megan smiled. This was Sam's first rodeo. She probably expected all the cowboys to be from the United States or Canada. In fact, a lot of people were surprised when they learned that Canadian cowboys were among the best in the world.

"Jack says you have Old Wally's buckle," said Megan.

Tony nodded. "I got it yesterday." He reached into his bag and pulled out an envelope. "I haven't had time to mount these and write up all the facts." He riffled through the papers and took a sheet out. "Here it is. Wally Deeze."

Megan looked at the rubbing. The belt buckle was oval. There was a rope pattern round the edge. In the centre was a design that looked like a 'D' with horns coming from the centre. The 'D' and horns were of the same rope design as the edging.

"I suppose it has that horn design in the middle because Wally used to ride bulls."

"What horns, Meg?" Tony looked puzzled.

"There." Megan pointed to the design coming from the letter D.

Tony smiled. "Those aren't horns. That's 'W' for Wally. Wally Deeze."

"Oh, now I see it." Samantha was peering over Megan's shoulder.

"What's Wally like?" asked Megan.

"Great," said Tony. "I was lucky to get one of the cowboys to help me talk to him in sign language. He can't talk."

Megan nodded. "He was born like that. But he got the limp when a bull trampled on his leg."

Tony looked surprised. "How do you know that?"

"This man told us." Megan turned round. But the man was no longer in the stands.

"Don had to leave," said a woman in a buckskin tasseled jacket. "He helps with the judging."

"Oh." Megan was disappointed. She'd hoped to hear what the man knew about Wally's brother. "Do you know anything about Wally's brother?" she asked.

The woman shook her head. "No, you'd have to ask Don. I think he knew both of them when they first came on the circuit."

"Oh." Megan was disappointed. She turned to Tony who was busy packaging his papers, putting them into envelopes. "I've got something to show you," she said. She looked round the stands. She didn't see anyone looking at her and she didn't have that creepy feeling. But she wanted to be sure. Everyone was concentrating on the arena.

Megan reached into her pocket. "Here." She took out the silver buckle in the palm of her hand.

"Wow! That's nice," said Tony. "Where'd you get that?"

"I found it on the ground," said Megan. "It was dropped by a man arguing with Old Wally."

"You mean they were arguing in sign language?"

Megan nodded. "Maybe it was the man who helped you talk to Wally. What was he like?"

"Well," Tony shrugged. "I didn't exactly take notice, but he was tall and . . ."

Megan cut in. "It couldn't be him. The man who was arguing with Wally was the same size as Wally."

Tony was holding out his hand. "Can I look, Meg?"

"Oh. I'm sorry, Tony. Sure." She held out the buckle. "Sam and I are taking it to the RCMP at the Safety Fair. We were there earlier but it was too busy and the duty officer was dealing with a theft from a car."

Ton gave the buckle back. "I'll have a look through my rubbings later. I know this buckle, but I've so many now I forget who they belong to."

"Then you'll be able to tell us whose buckle it is," said Samantha. "Hey! That'll be great. We'll have solved this mystery of yours, Megan."

"Mystery?" said Tony. "What mystery?"

Samantha was smiling. "Megan thinks there's something mysterious about this buckle," she said. "And after what happened I think there may be, too."

"After what happened?" Jack turned from watching the last bull rider. "What happened?"

Megan smiled. Her older brother couldn't resist a mystery and it would be nice to share this with the boys.

"I feel hungry," she said. "Let's get a hotdog or something and we'll tell you guys about it."

CHAPTER 9

Bound and Gagged

"I'M GLAD WE told the boys about the buckle," said Samantha. "They think there's something going on, too. Something mysterious."

Megan nodded. "It doesn't take much to make Jack think there's a mystery." She shivered.

"Are you cold?" asked Samantha.

The two friends were on their way back to the Petting Zoo. The sky was clouding over as evening drew in, but it wasn't cold. The heat of the day was trapped in the mass of tents and booths.

Megan shook her head. "No, but I had a funny feeling when we passed the trailers." She shivered again and stopped to look back. There was no sign of the clown.

"Come on, Meg." Samantha pulled at her sleeve. "We'll be late if we don't hurry."

It was true. Megan had lost track of time when they were talking to the boys. It was only when Jack said the rodeo events were over, and he and Tony must get to the stock pens to put out feed and fill the water troughs, that Megan realized how late it was. She hurried on. They'd agreed to meet Jack and Tony after this shift and go to the RCMP Tent together. Jack didn't want to be left out of that. Megan shivered again. There was nobody there so why did she have a scary feeling? There *was* a clown, but not the same one that had followed them before. This one had a black, felt top hat, a long black coat and pink pants. Was he following them, or was he just one of the midway entertainers. Did he look a little familiar? Megan didn't want to keep staring at him so she hurried on, but before she and Samantha entered the Petting Zoo she looked back. The clown was there, but he was talking to a family with five small children.

"You guys are late," said Jackie, an accusing look on her face.

"Sorry," said Samantha.

Megan looked at her watch. "We're only two minutes late," she said.

"Well, we relieved the two of you early," said Tara. "I told my mum I'd meet her at the Show Tent at six o'clock. Now she'll be mad."

Megan didn't reply. She didn't think Mum would be mad about a few minutes. Anyway, the rodeo was meant to be a fun time, not a time to get mad about little things.

"We'll come early tomorrow, if you want," said Samantha.

Tara shook her head. "Forget it. Come on, Jackie."

Megan shook her head as she watched the two girls hurry off. They hadn't even bothered to tell them if everything was all right; suppose a pet was sick? She wondered if they'd fed the animals for the night?

A man with a small girl approached.

"Are children allowed to ride the pony?" he asked.

"No. I'm sorry," said Megan. "I think he's good tempered, but he's only here to be petted."

"Oh." The man looked disappointed. "I told Shawna she could have a ride."

Megan looked at the little girl who couldn't be more than four. Her lips were quivering, her eyes filling with tears. Why had her father told her that? It was stupid. There were pony rides in the Midway. He should have taken her there.

"You can get rides at the fair," said Megan.

"I don't want to ride at the fair." The little girl shook her head. "I want to ride on that pony." She pointed at Billy.

Megan almost burst out laughing, but stopped herself in time. She could see Sam grinning, tiny fan lines forming at the outer corners of her dark, oval eyes.

"Well," said Megan. "Maybe Billy will let you sit on his back. Let's see." She opened the gate of Billy's pen. "Come on."

The little girl looked at her father. He nodded and she held Megan's hand. The tiny fingers were warm and damp.

"Billy, I want you to meet Shawna." Megan held Billy's collar. "Stroke him between his horns."

The little girl held her hand out, tentatively. She started to stroke Billy's head. He pulled back his lips in a silly grin.

"Daddy! He's smiling."

The man nodded. "I think that old goat likes you," he said.

"He's a pony, Daddy."

Megan smiled. "Let's see if Billy will let you sit on his back. There! Now hold onto his collar."

Billy looked round. He didn't kneel like he did to get Jack off his back. He stood there, looking as if he was bored.

"I want to tell Mummy. I want to tell Mummy."

Megan helped her get down.

"Thanks very much." The man smiled. "One day I'll have to explain the difference between ponies and goats, but not today."

Samantha was on the far side of the tent. As the man and the girl left she signaled to Megan. Megan was about to call out when her friend put a finger to her lips. She moved her head to the side, looking at the entrance, shaking her head slightly.

Megan looked and was just in time to see the clown in the top hat turn quickly and walk out of sight. He had been staring directly at her and now she knew why he looked familiar! His face makeup was the same! But that couldn't be right. She'd heard that no two clowns made up their faces the same way; it was a trademark.

Samantha hurried over. "Did you see him?"

Megan nodded. "He's the same clown we saw earlier, but he's wearing different clothes."

"What do you mean?"

Megan explained about the makeup.

The sooner we do something about that buckle the better," said Samantha. "I hope Mrs. Freeze is early. It's quite boring tonight. There aren't many people."

Megan agreed. It had been very slow. Children were at the fair with their parents. The Petting Zoo was busy during the day, but as evening fell the lights and sounds of the fair attracted people. Mrs. Freeze said the last two hours were always quiet.

Megan was worried. Mum had said not to get involved. Now she was in the middle of something that made her feel frightened. Absentmindedly she put her hand on Billy's head and scratched him behind his ears. Then she knew what to do. She looked towards the entrance. No one was there. Quickly she knelt down, took the buckle from her pocket and pushed it deep into the straw at the rear of Billy's bedding. She stood up and sighed. That felt better. Samantha was staring at her.

"I had to get rid of it . . . for now," said Megan. "Don't ask me why. I just didn't want it in my pocket."

It was dusk when the girls left the Petting Zoo. Lights from the Midway flashed red, yellow, blue and green, casting long, dark angular, moving shadows on the walls of booths and on the dusty walkways.

"I wish we'd told the boys to meet us at the tent," said Samantha.

"The Show tent isn't far now." Megan glanced back over her shoulder. She agreed with Samantha. As night fell the clash of sounds from the fair seemed to intensify and the flashing, coloured lights made the shadows move as if alive. She hurried on. It was lonely here, away from the bustle and activity of the Midway. There were horse trailers standing empty, dark and still, pickups, some old, some new, with license plates from many different places: Wyoming, Alberta, Manitoba, Montana, silent and squat, unnaturally quiet.

Before she knew what was happening Megan felt a strong hand pressed over her mouth. Other hands held her as a bag was pulled over her head. The cloth was rough and, by the smell, Megan knew it was a jute grain bag. She struggled but it was no use.

"Quit struggling!" The hand tightened over her mouth and her head was yanked roughly back. "Search her!" It was a young voice and cracked like Jack's. "And the other one."

Megan felt hands reach inside her pockets.

"Nothing, Rob."

"You dummy! I said 'no names.' Are you sure its not there?"

"Nothing here."

Megan was sure she'd heard that voice. Where? Was it one of the girls who'd been in the Petting Zoo when her bag was searched?

"He won't be happy about this," said the first. "He won't like it one bit."

Megan cringed as her head was yanked back again, this time by her hair. She wanted to cry out but the hand was still clamped over her mouth.

"Where is it?"

Briefly the hand was removed. Megan took a deep breath and was about to shout when the hand was clamped over her mouth once more.

"I'm going to ask you again. Nod your head if you know where the buckle is." The fingers in her hair were loosened. "Now, where is it."

Megan tried to bite the fingers pressing tightly against her mouth.

"Argh! You . . . Tie them up! Gag them!" The command was curt, the voice ugly with anger.

Megan couldn't believe it. These were just young kids, probably the same ones that had ransacked her bag. Rough hands pulled her arms behind her back and rope was lashed around her wrists. A gag was pushed into her mouth; it pressed the rough, dry cloth of the bag between her teeth. She thought she would choke as she fell face down, onto the hard dusty ground.

"Right. Let's go!"

The sound of running feet faded quickly as the young attackers got away. Then there was nothing but the background of music and laughter from the fair. Megan twisted and turned, eventually rolling onto her side. She knew Samantha was doing the same from the muffled grunts and groans nearby. Megan's wrists were tied so tightly that her hands were becoming numb. Why hadn't she asked the boys to meet them at the Petting Zoo? She had to get free! Mum and Dad would be here soon. What would Mum say?

CHAPTER 10

DeeDee and Fred

"NOW, YOU SAY the boys who attacked you were the same ones who tried to steal from your bags."

"Yes." Samantha nodded. "This afternoon at the Petting Zoo."

"We can't actually say that, Sam." Megan knew the boys were the same ones, but she couldn't prove it. "We didn't see them, I didn't, anyway. And I don't think it was just boys. I think two were girls."

About ten seconds after Megan had struggled to her feet and was straining to recover her breath through the gag, Tony and Jack had come running down the winding, dirt pathway beside the trailer parking area. Jack, as usual, was racing ahead of Tony. He tore round the bend and crashed into Megan. She thought she was being attacked again as she was knocked to the ground.

Now, seated in the police tent, sipping a hot cup of chocolate, she felt relieved. Constable Paduto had taken Samantha and herself to the St. John Ambulance tent. Megan liked Constable Paduto; she had dark hair cut short like Sam's, and dark brown eyes. Megan thought she was a bit small to be a police officer. Her hands and feet were so tiny.

"Well, I'm pleased the doctor gave you both a passing grade." The other police officer looked up from his notes. "Especially you, Megan."

Constable Paduto laughed. Her partner looked puzzled.

"What's so funny, Joan? It could have been very serious, so soon after a concussion. It was lucky that doctor was there."

Constable Paduto nodded. "I know, Vern. But you should have seen the St. John Ambulance guy's face. He couldn't believe his eyes. He was the one who treated Megan immediately after the bed race." She turned to Megan. "Why didn't you say you'd been injured in the bed races?"

Megan looked down into her mug of chocolate. "I didn't want to because Mum and Dad might stop me coming to the rest of the rodeo."

"They'll have to know."

Megan nodded. She'd been feeling better. Now she felt miserable. Mum and Dad hadn't arrived yet, but there would be trouble when they did.

Constable Paduto smiled. "Let me talk to them first. I'm sure they'll be only too pleased you're safe, and helping us with an investigation."

"That's just it," said Tony. "Mum hates it when we get involved in things."

"Is that why you didn't report the trouble in the Petting Zoo?" The policeman looked across from his desk.

"We did try," said Megan, "but the volunteers were busy and you weren't here because you were dealing with a theft from a car."

Constable Paduto smiled. "We weren't on duty at the time. Constable Sanders and I are on nights." She looked at her partner. "Rudi would have been on duty this afternoon, right, Vern?"

The officer nodded. He turned to Megan. "So you went to the arena, met Tony and Jack and then returned to work."

"Yes," said Megan. "That's when we saw the other clown, only he was the same one because of his makeup."

"Right. You explained that. But, maybe the Midway clowns have similar makeup." Constable Sanders looked towards the entrance of the RCMP tent. "Let's hope we can find those clowns soon."

Two volunteers had been sent to the Midway to look for the clowns. They said both were usually at the children's fair, amusing families out for a night of fun.

Constable Paduto went to the entrance. She looked out. "Here's Reg now." She stood back as a smiling volunteer came in followed by a clown wearing a black felt top hat and black coat with tails.

The clown smiled. "Hi! What's the problem?"

"These girls say you've been following them."

"Not him," said Megan. "He's much too tall."

The clown was very tall and very thin. He did have a black top hat and black coat with tails but his pants were bright green, and his makeup wasn't right.

"Let me introduce myself," said the clown. He raised his hat to reveal a shiny, bald, head with a rim of thin, straw-coloured, spiky hair. "I'm Dodo Drink-of-Water, DeeDee for short." He laughed, bowed low and looked round the tent. "I've always been tall and skinny and my friends used to say I was a long drink of water." He laughed again.

"But you did say the clown had a top hat and tails," said the volunteer. "DeeDee's the only one I know that dresses like that."

"That's right." DeeDee nodded. "I'm the only one working this rodeo with an outfit like this." He twirled his hat on one finger and flipped it into the air. It landed on his head. He turned to Samantha. "What time was it when you thought I was following you?"

"About six o'clock," said Samantha.

"This evening?"

Samantha nodded.

"About the time I was coming on duty." DeeDee smiled. "What part of the fair was that?"

"We weren't in the fair," said Megan. "We were walking through the Midway, past the booths."

"Wait!" said Constable Sanders. "We'll ask the questions." He looked at Megan. "Where did you see the clown?"

"By a cotton candy stall. And then outside the Petting Zoo." She shook her head. "But DeeDee isn't the one, his makeup is different."

"That's right." Constable Sanders nodded. "The makeup." He turned to DeeDee. "Do you and your partner . . . What's his name?"

"Fred," said DeeDee. "Roly Poly Fred."

"Thanks." The policeman made a note. "Now, do you and Fred make up your faces the same?"

"Oh, no." DeeDee shook his head. "A clown's face is part of his trademark."

There was the sound of laughter outside and the other volunteer entered the tent with a second clown. The clown wore a red and white polka dot shirt, red pants and a white, conical hat with a red pompom on the tip. He had a large, round, red nose. Megan knew immediately he wasn't the one. He was too short and too fat and, although he was laughing his makeup made him look sad.

Before anyone could speak, Megan shook her head. "It's not him."

"Why?" said Constable Sanders. "The makeup?"

Megan looked at the clown. "That's part of it. His makeup makes him look sad. The one we saw had a large, grinning mouth . . . and . . ."

"The short, fat clown laughed. There was a twinkle in his eyes. "Say it," he said. "I'm fat!"

Megan felt her face getting hot. She must be blushing. "I . . ."

"It doesn't bother me," said Roly Poly. "It's my name – Roly Poly Fred. If I wasn't small and fat I wouldn't be roly poly and I'd be out of work." He looked round. "So what's going on?"

Megan and Samantha explained again.

"You're right," said Fred. "No two clowns have exactly the same makeup." He scratched his head. "But what gets me is you say this clown wore two outfits, first a top hat and tails like DeeDee, and then a set like this, my outfit."

"And," said DeeDee, "I've been thinking."

"Don't strain yourself," said Fred. He burst out laughing.

To Megan it looked as if DeeDee started to grow. He stretched, standing very upright, looking down his pointed, white nose at Fred. "What I was going to say," he said slowly, "before I was so rudely interrupted, was that the only other clowns on this circuit, apart from old Wally and the Stooges, are Shamrock Pete and Corky. They're on day shift."

"That's true," said Fred. "But you've reminded me of something. Remember that time, about nine months back, DeeDe, when Shamrock Pete said he'd seen you early one morning?"

DeeDee nodded. "Right, Fred, at Calgary. Pete said he thought he'd seen me in the main parking lot. I was nowhere near it."

Megan was excited. "So what you're saying is someone could have been impersonating you?"

DeeDee nodded. "But why? Fred and I get paid to be here, to be on the circuit all year. Why would anyone do this for nothing?"

"Disguise," said Jack. "It's a disguise."

Megan had been wondering why Jack had been so quiet. Now she knew. He had obviously been thinking while they were talking.

"Suppose someone is doing something illegal or wrong and doesn't want to be seen," said Jack. "Well, if they are seen, like Meg and Sam saw this clown, the disguise will throw people off track."

"But what about the makeup?" said Megan. "The clown dressed like DeeDee had the same face as the one dressed like Fred."

DeeDee snapped his fingers. "She's right. Can you tell us what his makeup was like, maybe draw it? Fred and I might recognize it and be able to tell you who it is."

"Wow!" Megan felt so excited. "If you can tell us who it is we can solve the mystery of the buckle."

"Mystery?"

Megan felt her heart sink. It was Mum.

"What mystery? I thought I'd told you to keep your noses to yourselves, not to get involved in anything, especially you, Megan when you're just getting over that concussion."

Megan groaned inwardly. Mum would spoil her mystery. Tony and Jack had helped the police solve two mysteries, and she and Sam had helped with the mystery of the secret caves. She felt a headache coming.

"I've been searching all over for you," said Mum angrily. "After you left the Petting Zoo you were to stay at the Midway rides." Mum turned round. "You, too, Jack, and you, Tony."

"But we're helping the police, Mum," said Tony.

That did it. Mum's eyes flashed steely blue.

"We're just helping, Mum." Megan looked round for support. "We're not really involved."

"That's not what I heard." Mum strode across the tent, that angry look on her face. "I was told that two girls were found bound and gagged." She stopped dead, her eyes wide, hand to mouth. "Oh, Megan, just look at you. You're injured."

Megan felt Mum's arm round her shoulders. It was comforting, but . . .

"Your face! It's grazed!" Mum's voice was rising. "Who did this? What did they do to you?"

Constable Paduto stepped forward. "We don't know, Mrs. Perry, not yet. But you can be sure we'll find them. And the girls are okay, that was the first thing we checked. A doctor was visiting the St. John Ambulance tent. He gave them both a thorough examination."

"But who attacked them?"

"Kids, Mum."

"Kids? What kids?"

Constable Paduto explained.

"But how can anyone so young do this?" Mum shook her head. "I don't understand."

"There are a lot of children less fortunate than yours, Mrs. Perry." Constable Sanders sighed. "We see them all the time; kids whose parents don't care. They have nothing to do. They join gangs to feel part of something. And then there are the ones who are runaways. They end up on the street."

Mum shook her head. "I know what you are saying. We see it in the newspapers, on television. I don't know what the world is coming to."

Constable Paduto smiled. "Well, you should be thankful to have such good kids, Mrs. Perry. And they are being a great help to us. This really is a mystery."

"Mystery!" Mum's eyes flashed steely blue again.

Why did the police officer say that word? The mention of the word 'mystery' made Mum mad. A minute ago Mum was calming down. Megan sighed. Now Mum was uptight again.

"Always getting involved with mysteries." Mum shook her head looking at Megan. "How will Dad explain this to Mr. Liang?"

"Leave that to us, Mrs. Perry," said Constable Sanders. "We'll explain to Mr. and Mrs. Liang."

"What I mean," said Mum, "is that this is not the first time my children have involved Samantha in something best left to the RCMP."

"I understand." The police officer looked first at Megan then Samantha. "We'll make sure none of them get involved any more than is necessary. But, as my partner says, we want to find out what is going on here."

Mum shook her head, her lips pressed tightly together. She closed her eyes for a moment and Megan heard her breathing in and out through her nose. It was Mum's way of trying to stay calm. "How soon can I take them home?"

Constable Sanders looked at his notes. "Constable Paduto and I have two things we want to do, Mrs. Perry. First we'd like Megan to give us a description of this clown. And we need to recover the buckle from the Petting Zoo. That will be it for tonight."

He turned to his partner. "Joan, while Megan gives me the description, why don't you go to the Petting Zoo with Samantha?"

"Good idea, Vern. That'll save time." Constable Paduto looked at Mum. "Is that okay with you, Mrs. Perry?"

Mum nodded. "Anything to get this over and done with. The sooner I get them home the better."

"Tony should come with us," said Samantha. "Billy might not like being disturbed."

Megan looked at her friend. Sam wasn't scared of Billy, was she?

"I'm not scared of Billy," said Samantha. "It's just that he won't move sometimes and . . ."

"You're right," said Tony. "Billy might get a bit upset. And I haven't seen the old beast for a couple of days. I'd better go."

CHAPTER 11

A Clown's Face

MEGAN SAT AT the metal, gray-painted RCMP desk. She'd been given a pencil, and some crayons from a Safety Fair children's package. Drawing the clown's face was more difficult than she'd thought. First she started with the eyes. That didn't work. She wished Mum would stop pacing up and down. She turned the paper over and started again, this time with the mouth. It was not an evenly shaped mouth; on the right side was a point; on the left it was rounded, giving it a lopsided look. The upper lip had a large M shape in the middle, like the M in a McDonald's restaurant sign, only it was red and not yellow. The lower lip stretched in a long loop halfway down the chin. Megan licked her own lips. Yes. That was good.

Mum had stopped by the entrance to the tent. Tony and Samantha had been gone for a while, but they should be back soon. Jack was talking to the policeman. Megan looked down at the paper on the desk before her.

The nose was easy, a big, round red ball; and the marks on the cheeks were easy, too, three red lines at an angle, sloping down and inwards on either side. Back to the eyes. Then she remembered: there were lines coming down from the eyebrows through the eyes and down to just above the cheeks. The lines weren't tears but gave that impression, so the face had both a happy and sad look. And the greasepaint round each eye looked like giant, white commas lying on their sides.

"That looks good." Constable Sanders stood by the desk, looking over Megan's shoulder. Jack was by his side.

"It's really great, Meg. I didn't know you could draw so well."

Megan felt good. It really was a good likeness of the clown, and praise from Jack was rare. "I have to put in some hair." She sketched in some yellow lines above the face and down the sides. "It wasn't real hair," she said. "It was a wig."

"DeeDee! Fred! Come over here!" The policeman beckoned to the clowns who were talking with the volunteers.

Megan finished drawing the hair. She was pleased that the face had turned out all right. Then she shivered. It was her own drawing, but the face gave her that same creepy, scared feeling.

"What's the matter, Meg?"

Megan hadn't noticed Mum come over. Mum put a hand on Megan's forehead.

"You're not getting another fever, are you?" She shook her head. "No. But you should be in bed."

"I'm not tired, Mum. But it's getting a little cooler now and I haven't got my coat on."

Megan reached behind her for her bag and pulled out her jacket. If Mum thought she was suffering from concussion again there'd be no rodeo tomorrow. She smiled as Fred and DeeDee came up to the desk. The clowns looked so funny, one a fat round ball, the other tall and thin. Megan could see why DeeDee's friends had called him a long drink of water.

"Do you recognize that face?" asked Constable Sanders.

DeeDee peered down from above and Fred looked sideways.

"It's not someone I know," said DeeDee. "Its' not Shamrock Pete or Corky, that's for sure."

"No, that's right, DeeDee," Fred studied the drawing. "But . . ." he paused. "You know, I can't tell you what it is, but there is something vaguely familiar about it."

"You mean you recognize it?"

"I didn't say that." Fred shook his head, the red pompom on his hat swinging from side to side. "As DeeDee said, it's not Pete or Corky." He shook his head. "Give me a while to think." He stared at the paper. "No. Won't come. But there is something . . ." He picked up the drawing and studied it. "Sorry." He shook his head. "It won't come."

Megan was disappointed. She was sure the face was right and she'd really wanted to solve the mystery. She looked at it again. It really did give her the shivers.

"Maybe if I sleep on it," said Fred. "I often remember things after a good sleep. And, talking of sleep . . ." He took an enormous gold watch from his pocket. "DeeDee. We're off duty now." He looked at the policeman.

Megan looked at her own watch. Almost eleven o'clock. Wow! It was really late.

Constable Sanders called to the volunteers. "Do you know where to find DeeDee and Fred if we need them?"

The first volunteer nodded. "Are you guys parked in your usual place?"

"Yep!" said Fred. "Down by the old stables. I'm at the far end of section 'A'. DeeDee's three trailers down."

"Okay." Constable Sanders nodded. "Thanks for your help. As soon as you remember anything get up here right away."

"I'll do that." Fred smiled.

The two were walking away when the policeman called after them. "Hold it! I almost forgot. Do either of you know how to sign?"

"Sign?" said DeeDee. "Oh! You mean like speak in sign language?" He shook his head. "Never could learn it myself."

"No," said Fred. "I couldn't either."

"Mm. Anyone you know who can? We'll need to speak to Old Wally as early as possible tomorrow."

"One of the pickup men signs," said Jack. "Tony told me he helped him when he got Old Wally's buckle rubbing."

"That's right," said Fred. "That will be Skipper Tompkins. He's a friend of Wally's. They've been on the circuit together for years. Skipper can sign."

"Where do we find Skipper?"

"He and Larry Zyg stay at a bed and breakfast, don't they, DeeDee?"

"That's right." DeeDee nodded. "The Tuck Inn B & B. It's close by and they say the breakfasts are even better than the rodeo pancake breakfast."

"I know the place," said Constable Sanders. "The breakfasts are great. Good coffee, too. It's run by Betty Voss."

DeeDee nodded. "Is that it? Can we go?"

"Yes, and thanks again for your help."

The clowns started to walk away, but at the entrance to the tent they turned, looked at each other and bowed. Together they said: "Goodnight, all."

Megan laughed. They looked so funny. It was hard for Fred to bow. DeeDee just seemed to fold in half. But the mention of food had reminded her she was hungry. She wished Tony and Samantha were back. Mum would have hot chocolate and doughnuts when they got home.

"The sooner I get you children to bed the better I'll be pleased," Mum looked at her watch. "Look at the time!"

Megan sighed. Why couldn't Mum lighten up. The policeman was trying to be friendly and he had to do his job. Then she heard voices outside the tent. One voice was Samantha's.

As Tony entered the tent Megan knew something was wrong.

"It wasn't there," said Samantha. She looked really upset.

Megan couldn't believe her ears. The buckle was gone!

"We searched everywhere, Meg." Tony picked a piece of straw from the sleeve of his checkered shirt. "It just wasn't there. I took Billy out in the end and we pulled his bedding apart and sifted through it. If it was there we'd have found it."

There was silence. Megan felt that everyone in the RCMP tent was staring at her. Did they believe her? She looked round. Samantha looked as if she was about to cry. Megan felt like crying, too. Tony was looking glum. The police officers were looking at her, waiting. The only person who didn't look upset was Mum.

"Well, that's that." Mum was smiling. "The person who lost it obviously saw you hide it, Meg and took it back. Why he couldn't ask for it in the first place I don't know." She shook her head. "It's over."

"But it's not over, Mum. That's just it." Megan couldn't believe that Mum seemed to have forgotten that she and Sam had been attacked. She looked from Constable Sanders to Constable Paduto for support. "Don't you see? Why did those guys come to the Petting Zoo and empty our bags? Why did the clown keep following us. And why were we attacked and tied up? There has to be a mystery."

Mum sighed and shook her head. Her lips were pressed tightly together and she looked tired. Why did Mum and Dad work themselves so hard? Meg hoped it wasn't because they wanted a big, modern, new house. If only Dad had time to build Mum an office, of her own.

"I just wanted to forget the whole thing," said Mum. "I don't want any more mysteries." Her lips quivered.

Constable Paduto came over to the desk and looked at Megan's drawing. "Unfortunately, Megan is right, Mrs. Perry. The girls were attacked. We have to find this clown." She looked at her partner. "Did DeeDee or Fred recognize the clown?"

Constable Sanders shook his head. "No, but Fred had a feeling the face was familiar. He may come up with something tomorrow." He nodded. "I suggest everyone go home and get some sleep."

Megan knew he was right. With the excitement of the day, and now the loss of the buckle, she was feeling very tired. But something was nagging her, some thought that wouldn't come. What was it? She shrugged. Maybe Fred was right. Sleep on it.

CHAPTER 12

The Silver Buckle

MEGAN WOKE EARLY. A narrow band of sunlight was streaming into her room through a gap in the drapes. She smiled. Mum still called the drapes, curtains, though it was years since she and Dad had come to Canada. That was before Megan was born. And Mum still called cookies, biscuits, as did Mrs. Liang. Even though the Liangs were from South Africa, Mum and Samantha's mother could talk for hours about Marie biscuits, joints of meat instead of roasts, sweets instead of candies, and all sorts of other things. Dad was the same: sometimes he called the trunk of a car, the boot.

Megan stretched and then lay back, her head on her pillow. She watched the tiny flecks of dust dancing in the stream of light. The specks of dust looked like miniature shreds of silver and gold. She pursed her lips and blew gently. The tiny particles rolled over and over, swirling this way and that.

Gradually, the events of the previous night started to flow back. The buckle had gone from Billy's stall. It had vanished. But, what was it she had tried to remember as she fell asleep last night? Suddenly she sat up. Mrs. Freeze! That was it! Mrs. Freeze! If Billy's stall had been dirty Mrs.Freeze would have cleaned it! She jumped out of bed and flung open her bedroom door. She raced down the hall to the room Jack and Tony shared.

"Jack! Slow down!" Mum's voice was raised. "I'd like a lie-in without you disturbing the household."

Megan turned and went quietly to the door of her parent's bedroom. She knocked gently.

"What now? Who is it? Oh, come in."

Megan turned the old coloured glass handle and opened the door just enough to poke her head inside the room. "It was me, Mum, not Jack."

Mum sat up, resting on her elbows. She looked sideways at the old alarm clock. "Do you have any idea what time it is, Megan?"

"No, Mum."

"It's only just gone six." Mum sighed. "What on earth has got into you? Are you all right?"

"Yes, Mum. I just woke up and it's such a lovely day."

Mum looked over at the window. "Yes, I can see that." She yawned. "But you get back to bed for an hour. I really don't think that bang on the head did you any good."

Megan sighed. "Yes, Mum." She closed the door, holding the handle, letting the latch click gently into place.

As she turned back down the hall the door of the boys' room opened. Jack looked out. Megan put a finger to her lips. She tiptoed down the hall, hoping the floorboards wouldn't creak.

"Let's go in," she whispered.

Tony was still fast asleep, his mouth open, his right arm outstretched, his hand hanging limply over the edge of the bed.

"What's up?" said Jack as he pushed the door to.

"I remembered what bothered me last night. It was Mrs. Freeze."

Jack looked puzzled. "What about Mrs. Freeze?"

"Remember?" said Megan. "She's at the Petting Zoo every night, from eight o'clock until sometime after closing at ten. If it's slow she cleans out the stalls before ten so she can get away early. Tony and Sam didn't say they'd seen her or Ron when they went to look for the buckle. It was really slow when Sam and I were on duty. I bet it stayed slow and Mrs. Freeze left early. We have to ask her if she cleaned out Billy's stall."

Jack pursed his lips and whistled softly. "And did she find the buckle? It's possible, Meg. But why are you keeping this so hush-hush? We should tell Mum and Dad."

Megan put a hand on her brother's arm as he went to open the door. "Wait, Jack! Mum's upset about Sam and I being attacked. And now she's angry with me for banging my door and waking her."

Jack grinned. "You're taking after me, eh?"

Megan shook her head. "I was so excited, thinking of Mrs. Freeze cleaning the stalls that I didn't think of the time. It's only just gone six and Mum said to go back to bed for an hour."

Jack sighed. "Well, we'd better do that. As you said, Mum's upset enough as it is. Better not set her up for the rest of the day."

Megan tossed and turned in her bed. This was stupid. She didn't have a good book to read because they hadn't been to the library this weekend. And she couldn't get back to sleep thinking of the buckle and where it might be. Suppose Mrs. Freeze had it, or Ron. That wouldn't be so bad. They could get it back and give it to the police. But suppose the Freezes had cleaned out Billy's stall and tipped the buckle, with the old, dirty straw, onto the manure pile? Where did Jack say the manure was? Oh, yes: behind the stock pens near the barns.

And suppose, because it was dark, Ron and Mrs. Freeze hadn't seen the buckle, and now it was lying there gleaming in the sun. Anyone could have found it, perhaps the clown!

Megan was getting a headache thinking of all the things that could have gone wrong. Suppose the buckle had dropped out of the wheelbarrow as the dirty straw was wheeled away? Suppose . . . No she didn't want to think of any more possibilities.

"Meg! Time to get up!" Mum was calling from downstairs.

Megan struggled up in bed. She must have fallen off to sleep. Her head felt awful, but she couldn't say anything, Mum would make her stay at home. She moved her head slowly from side to side and then up and down. It wasn't a headache like the one she had after the bed crashed. That was good. This was a worry headache.

She slid her feet into her slippers and padded down the hall to the bathroom. Good. It was empty. It smelled all steamy and warm and there was a mixture of the perfumed smell of Mum's creamy soap and the medicine smell of Dad's 'sensible' soap. Dad said it was antiseptic.

The mirror on the medicine cabinet was not quite clear of steam. Megan slid the door open. They were there. Should she take one or two pills? One should be fine.

Five minutes later she was at the kitchen table. "You're very quiet this morning, Meg," said Dad.

Megan chewed her pancake. She felt guilty about taking a pill for her headache and not telling. The pancake didn't need chewing but it gave her time to think. And chewing was good, as Mum's pancakes were even better than at the rodeo.

"I'm enjoying the pancakes, Dad."

"Me too." Dad smiled. "The rodeo breakfasts are good, but Mum's are the best." Dad poured syrup on another pancake. "And this Maple syrup is much better than the pancake syrup at the rodeo."

Megan agreed. Maple syrup was the best. It had a very special taste.

"And another thing," said Dad. "The breakfast this morning will be crowded; it always is on a Sunday, with families going to the Cowboy Church service. And look at the weather. Incredible!"

Megan looked out of the kitchen window. It was a beautiful day. She smiled. Two of the geese were breakfasting on lush grass by the stream. The grass reminded her of part of the *Cowboy's Prayer* she'd heard last year at the Sunday service in the arena. It went something like '*the last ride to the big country up there, where the grass grows lush and green and stirrup high.*' She couldn't remember any more.

Megan liked the part about the grass being stirrup high. She could imagine ghostly cowboys high in their saddles, riding through a sea of waving grass brushing against their leather boots.

One of the geese trumpeted. There was only one goose nesting this year. Megan wiped her plate clean with the last piece of pancake.

She wondered if they'd have goslings. Last year two geese had sat for ages, well past hatching time. Finally, Dad told Jack and Tony to remove the eggs as they were obviously infertile.

It had been a lovely day, but windy. The boys carried the eggs down behind the barn. Tony dropped one. The smell was terrible. Then Jack had an idea. He and Tony placed the eggs in a long line. They stood some distance away and threw rocks at them. The rotten smell was carried by the wind across the road to Mrs. Tandy's garden. Megan could still hear that high-pitched shriek as the old lady ran to her house.

"What are you smiling at, Meg?"

Dad's question broke the spell of the daydream. Megan hadn't realized she'd been smiling.

"I was remembering last year, Dad, when the boys broke all those eggs."

"Well, we don't want a repeat of that." Dad shook his head. "I was sick to my stomach. And Mrs. Tandy went on and on for weeks. Anyway, time to get cleared up."

The boys had already cleared their plates and mugs and were helping Mum at the sink.

Megan hoped they could get to the rodeo soon. She wanted to know what the police had found out. Had they spoken to old Wally? And she wanted to speak to Mrs. Freeze. Dad had telephoned Mrs. Freeze this morning but Ron said she was out for the day. However, he did say his mum had cleaned some stalls and he thought Billy's was one of them. But she hadn't said anything about a buckle.

Megan reached for Dad's plate. He looked at her and put his hand on hers.

"Remember what Mum said." He looked serious. "I still can't believe a group of youngsters would attack you two like that, but these days it seems anything can happen. So, leave all this mystery business to the police. Right?"

Megan nodded. Dad was right, but it was all so frustrating, not knowing anything. But at least her headache was gone.

CHAPTER 13

An Important Letter

"NO, I DON'T expect to see them this morning. They were on late last night."

Megan couldn't believe it. She couldn't wait a whole day to see Constable Paduto or her partner. What was going on? And what about telling them about Mrs. Freeze? She looked at the volunteer.

"Didn't they leave a message?" she said.

"Are you one of the Perry children?"

Megan nodded. "I'm Megan."

"Ah." The volunteer opened a drawer in the desk and took out a buff-coloured envelope. "Yes. Here it is. Joan Paduto made a note in our instructions for this to be given to you."

"Thank you."

The volunteer held out another envelope. "Are your parents here?"

"Not here," said Megan. "Mum and Dad are at the Products Building. They're going to spend some time there before going to the rodeo performance. I'm off to work at the Petting Zoo."

The volunteer nodded and returned the envelope to the desk drawer. "When you see them please tell them I have this here and for . . ."

"Mr. and Mrs. Liang?" asked Megan.

"Right." The man smiled.

Megan turned. She wanted to get away. Her heart beat faster as she looked at the envelope. It was addressed to her but Jack was outside. He was waiting for a juggler who was to perform soon. She looked towards the entrance to the tent. Tony was at the Show tent but he'd be back soon, and before anyone else saw the letter she wanted to read it herself. She poked her head out of the tent. There was a large crowd now. She couldn't see the boys or the juggler, but rising and spinning alternately above the mass of heads were balls, clubs and plates. Jack would be at the front, hidden from her sight by the taller people. There was still no sign of Tony. Megan tore open the envelope hurriedly. Inside was a single sheet of paper folded in four. She unfolded it. At the top was the RCMP crest; under that the date and time, late last night.

Dear Megan,

I know you will want to know if anything has arisen concerning the buckle. We have no results at this time. (Midnight.)

We tried to contact Wally Deeze before going off duty. He was not at his trailer and was probably at the Ten-Gallon Hat saloon, the Casino or one of the country shows.

I did manage to contact Larry Zyg, the friend of Skipper Tompkins, at the Tuck Inn B & B. Tompkins was out, probably with Deeze. I asked Zyg to have Tompkins tell Wally we need to talk with him. Tompkins will give me a call to arrange a convenient time to meet with them. I'll let you know what happens.

If you or Tony have any more thoughts about the buckle, or the clown's makeup, please leave a message with the volunteers or officer on day shift. They can contact us as necessary. If you see the clown that followed you do not approach him. Report to the RCMP tent.

We have left a similar note for DeeDee and Fred in case Fred recalls what was familiar about the face you drew.

We would also like you and Samantha to keep your eyes open for the kids who emptied your bags. Again, do not approach them. Get a good look if you can and note description, clothing etc.

I will let you know what progress is made and will keep your parents informed.

Joan Paduto
Constable, RCMP

Megan quickly read the note again, refolded it, put it in the envelope and tucked it in her jeans pocket. She looked at her watch. Twenty minutes until her noon shift with Samantha. There was just enough time to go to the barns and search the manure pile. She'd get Jack and Tony to come.

She pushed her way to the front of the crowd. There was no sign of the boys. Maybe Jack had gone to the Show Tent, too. As she pushed her way back through the crowd people complained. Some took advantage of others who let her through. They pushed in to get a better look. Where were the boys? Maybe they weren't at the Show Tent. Maybe they'd left early for work at the stockyards? They were supposed to stay with her and take her to the Petting Zoo. Maybe they'd gone there? What if they'd pushed their way out of the crowd as she was pushing her way to the front to find them? They wouldn't have seen her and maybe thought she'd gone to work. If they went to the RCMP tent the volunteer would say that's where she'd gone.

Megan ran to the Petting Zoo. The boys weren't there, neither was Samantha. She looked at her watch: fifteen minutes. She shouldn't really go by herself, but it wouldn't take long to have a quick look.

CHAPTER 14

Front End Loader

THERE WASN'T JUST one manure pile, there were lots; huge piles of straw and animal droppings. Each pile was beginning to send off steam, heated by the midday sun overhead. There was a strong, pungent smell. Megan sighed. She should have guessed. With all the animals at the rodeo there wouldn't be just one pile.

The manure piles weren't actually in the stable area but in the city works yard behind the barns, behind a chain-link fence. Beyond the manure were rows of heavy machinery: graders, fork lifts, front-end loaders, cherry pickers and dump trucks. All were painted bright yellow. There was a chain-link double gate secured with an enormous padlock

Megan could understand why the machinery was locked up, but why lock up the manure? She shrugged and shook her head. It was useless. She didn't have time to find a way in and have a look. Anyway, if the gate had been locked, how would Mrs. Freeze get rid of the straw? Maybe this wasn't the place.

As she was about to leave Megan heard a car stop close behind her. She turned. Two men in orange-coloured coveralls got out.

"Can I help?" asked the driver. He was about Dad's age and had smiling blue eyes beneath thick, dark eyebrows.

The other man waved and walked to the gate. Keys jangled on a long chain attached to his belt.

"I lost something in the Petting Zoo yesterday," said Megan, "in one of the stalls."

"You mean you think it's in one of those piles?" The man removed an orange and white striped hardhat and scratched his curly dark hair. He smiled and shook his head. "You'll never find it."

"It might not be here," said Megan. "It depends on when the gates are locked."

"Eleven," said the man. "We have to lock up the machinery, of course, because of vandals, but you'd be surprised at the trouble we had in past years with people stealing manure."

"Stealing manure?" Megan couldn't believe it.

"Yes. They'd come in pickups and take a load; didn't care how much mess they spread around, they were in such a hurry not to be caught. It took us hours to clean up. So now we have the rodeo we pile it behind the fence."

"Oh, I see." Megan shook her head. Dad said some people could be dirty and uncaring.

The man smiled. "Anyway, this thing you lost, I don't see how you expect to find it in all that."

"Could I have a look?" Megan decided to use her pleading tone. "Just a quick look? Please?" She heard the sound of a diesel engine fire into life. In the works yard a puff of black smoke came from the vertical exhaust of a front-end loader.

"Well, I don't know." The city worker looked at his watch. "We've been given four hours to move as much as we can."

Megan couldn't believe it. They were going to move the manure! The diesel engine throbbed and she saw the steel tracks of the loader begin to turn and roll as the machine started to grind its way across the yard. A huge steel scoop swayed back and forth as the machine moved forward.

"No!" Shouted Megan. "Stop!"

The city worker grabbed her arm as she started to run forward. "Hey! Hold it!"

"But it will be lost." Megan felt like crying. Why hadn't she thought about Mrs. Freeze last night? Why hadn't she thought to call Constable Paduto today? The police would have searched the area.

"This thing you lost. Is it valuable?"

Megan hadn't thought about the buckle being valuable, but it had to be if the clown was so intent on getting it.

"Yes." She nodded. "It's not mine, but I lost it and the police want it back."

"Mm." The man scratched his head again. "So, it's valuable and the police want it?" He looked at his watch. "Is there a reward? Is that why you're so eager to find it?"

"No." Megan looked back to the yard.

The huge scoop was dipping down slowly into the front of a nearby pile of manure. The scrape of metal against the blacktop of the works yard set Megan's teeth on edge.

"No! No! He's got to stop. We must find it!"

The man appeared to make a decision. He raised his left arm, holding his hard hat high, waving it from side to side. "Jake!" He shook his head. "He'll never hear me." He ran towards the gate. Megan followed.

The arm of the front-end loader rose up, the scoop full. The machine turned and trundled away to a dump truck nearby. The scoop tilted, sending a shower of straw and manure into the steel box. The machine turned.

The city worker was waving both arms now, the orange and white paint of his hat gleaming in the sun. "Hey! Jake!"

The machine stopped. The driver leaned out of the cab. "What's up?"

The other man shouted back. "Shut her down, Jake." He turned to Megan. "You're not having me on about the police wanting this thing, are you?"

Megan shook her head. The yard went quiet as the engine of the machine spluttered and stopped.

"What's this about, Mac?" the driver asked as he approached.

"Yeah." Mac looked at Megan. "What exactly are we looking for?"

"A silver buckle," said Megan. "An old one."

"You mean a championship buckle?"

Megan looked at Mac. Could he be right? He had to be. It must be valuable, and the man she'd seen arguing with Old Wally must have stolen it.

"Some old buckles are worth a fortune," said Jake. "I was looking at the vintage collection in the Show Tent, yesterday. The history behind some of them is really something. But, how come you're looking for one here?"

Megan briefly explained.

Jake shook his head. "It can't be from the Show tent, they're locked up and each buckle is set in a velvet backing. If one was stolen it would stick out like a sore thumb. But it sure is a mystery. Like you say."

"It's a mystery all right." Mac scratched his head. "But let's see if we can find it. Mind you, it'll be like searching for a needle in a haystack. Which is the latest pile, Jake?"

"The one I started on. Over there." Jake looked thoughtful. "Now wait a minute! Hold it! I scooped the first load from the bottom of the pile, right?" He sounded excited. "Did you say this woman who cleans the stalls uses a wheelbarrow?"

Megan nodded. "Yes. Mrs. Freeze."

"Right." Jake smiled. "If I was your Mrs. Freeze I'd dump the muck on the nearest pile, that one, the new one." He pointed to the pile where the front-end loader stood idle.

"I'm with you, Jake," said Mac. "And she'd just tip it on the bottom, where you scooped first."

"Right." Jake turned. "Come on!" He ran over to the dump truck. Give me a hand up!"

Mac pushed as Jake scrambled up into the truck and slid over the lip of the box. "Phew!" Jake's voice sounded hollow and muffled. "It stinks in here." There were scraping sounds and the banging of heavy boots on thick metal. Then there was silence. A minute went by and then another. Silence.

Megan looked up at the truck. What was happening? She turned to Mac. He was frowning.

"What's he doing in there?" Mac shook his head. "It was only one scoop."

As if in answer, Jake's head appeared over the rim of the box. He was grinning and, as Megan watched, he slowly raised his right hand high. The sun glinted on a shining silver buckle.

"Bingo!" Jake heaved himself onto the rim of the box. "Thought I'd keep you in suspense." He scrambled down the side and jumped to the ground. "It certainly is a nice old buckle; pretty worn, though; a lot of letters are half rubbed out." He looked at it again and passed it to Megan.

"Thank you," she said. "This is it." Megan's heart was beating fast. "I'm taking it straight to the RCMP tent." She turned to go, then turned back. "Thanks a bunch."

Mac grinned. "You're welcome. Now, remember. If there's a reward, it was us who helped you. Right?" He shook his head as Jake started to laugh.

"Always an eye for a dollar, eh, Mac?"

"Just kidding," said Mac. "Just kidding. Do you want one of us to go with you?"

Megan shook her head. "I'll be okay, thanks. It's not far." She smiled. "Thanks again for your help."

CHAPTER 15

A Clown in Green

A S SHE RAN out of the works yard Megan glanced at her watch. Oh, no! It was almost half past twelve. Samantha would be on her own, wondering where she was. Behind her she heard the diesel engine of Jake's machine roar into life once more. Then another engine spluttered and started throbbing in unison. Megan thought Mac and Jake should wear masks. She still had the smell of manure in her nostrils.

The shortest route to the Safety Fair would be through the main parking area. But was that the quickest way? There were masses of cars and trucks and people coming and going. That would slow her down. The best way would be directly through the barns. She veered right and came to the rows of red trimmed, white, corrugated sheathed buildings. The sunlight reflected off the white siding was almost blinding. She grasped the buckle tightly. It was really quite heavy.

Above the noise of the machines in the works yard Megan heard a horse whinny nearby. A stable hand was busy filling a bucket with feed from a container. He looked up. Megan knew that stable hands had to be sixteen or older. They were usually small, but this one was shorter than Tony. He waved and shouted something as she ran past, but the words were lost in the roar of diesel engines.

Megan waved back, thinking as she ran. The man at the works yard was probably right. This had to be a special buckle, or why would anyone attack her and Sam to get it back. She shivered. Maybe she should have asked one of the men to come with her.

She had made her way to the right but now, on either side two long, narrow white barns seemed to stretch on and on and, at the far end there was another building. Was it joined to the others? Did it block the exit? Maybe the stable hand had been shouting to tell her that. She looked back. He was waving, pointing to the right. Ah! There were two barns, not one long one. Megan waved back.

The gap was narrow and it was quite dark here after the bright sunlight. The gable-ended sides of the barns were painted a flat, dark red, like the trim of the doors and windows. The colour made the alley between the two seem even darker. That's why she hadn't noticed it. Ahead was another sunlit courtyard between more barns and, on the far side another alley like the one she was in.

A figure appeared at the far end of the alley opposite. Megan could see it was a clown, but not dressed in red or white, or in black tails and top hat. Maybe it was Corky or Shamrock Pete, one of the other Midway clowns. The clown looked left and right and then backed into the alley, pausing for a moment. Then he turned and hurried towards the courtyard.

Megan pressed herself flat against the wall of the barn. She didn't know why she was frightened, but she was.

The clown paused again when he reached the courtyard. He peered out of the alley, looking to the left and right. Megan held her breath, trembling; it was him, the same face, only this time he was wearing a green and white striped shirt, a very wide green tie and a green plastic hat like people wore on St. Patrick's Day. The colours were so bright that she'd almost missed his face. With a final look to the right the clown hurried out of view, turning left.

Megan breathed out slowly and crept forward, careful not to make a sound. The bright sunlight in the courtyard had probably saved her from being seen in the deep shadow. She reached the end of the alley and slowly, carefully, looked out to the left. She was just in time. Halfway down, on the opposite side of the yard, a green clad figure was opening a door. He started to turn and Megan barely had time to pull her head back. She held her breath, her heart thumping. She counted slowly to twenty.

She had reached 'fourteen' when she heard a door close. She waited and then slowly looked out again. Above the door the clown had entered was a wooden sign: *LONE STAR ENTERPRISES*. The letters were carved, painted yellow, and there was a five-pointed star at each end.

Megan tensed, then, with a bound, she sprinted out of hiding, across the yard into the alley on the other side. She stopped, breathing heavily, and looked out quickly. Nothing! She hadn't been seen. Wow! If she'd run that fast at the spring track meet she'd have won. She looked back – still clear. Ahead was the trailer parking lot and, above the trailers, in the distance, the tree where Sam and she had stood. Was that only yesterday?

Then she had an idea. The Show Tent was much closer than going all the way to the Safety Fair and the RCMP tent. And Constable Paduto and Constable Sanders wouldn't be on duty yet. She ran on, dodging between trailers until she reached the clearing and the Show Tent.

"Wait up!" The security guard at the entrance put out a hand. "Where'd you think you're going?"

"To see the Vintage Buckle exhibit." Megan looked over her shoulder. Why was this man stopping her?

"You can't just go in, you know."

Then Megan remembered. She reached into her shirt pocket and pulled out her pass.

"You're meant to wear that all the time."

"Sorry." Megan slipped the string over her head. "I forgot when I got dressed this morning."

The man smiled. "Okay, but keep it on, right."

Megan nodded and stepped into the tent. There weren't many people. She looked round. Which one was the curator? Everyone was wearing rodeo gear like she was.

In the centre of the tent was a wooden showcase with a glass top. A group was gathered round.

"Look at that one, Dad." A boy of about Jack's age pointed into the case.

"It looks like a real oldie." The man shook his head. "Trust me to forget my glasses. What does the card say?"

"Wow! It says it's sixty two years old. The first person to win it was someone called Dusty Mathers. It's for bull riding, and the last time it was won was in nineteen fifty-eight, the year they started the Vintage Collection. The winner donated it."

Megan pressed forward and squeezed between a fat lady and a thin man. The man looked down his nose at Megan and she purposely avoided his eyes and concentrated on the display. There were a lot of buckles, some with centrepieces of bull riding, some of saddle-bronco riders, others with chuck wagon teams and others steer wrestling. A few had a date on the buckle, and the word *CHAMPION*.

Then she saw it, on the far side. It was a heavily worn buckle. In the centre was a scene of a bronco, its back arched, a rider holding on. The lettering was so worn it was difficult to read. Slowly, Megan inched her way to the far side of the cabinet. The silver buckle was still clasped in her left hand. All the way from the works yard she'd held it so tightly that now, as she opened her hand, her fingers felt stiff and numb. She looked down.

How could there be two? It was impossible!

Megan stared through the thick, plate glass top of the showcase. Nestled in black velvet was her buckle, or at least, one that looked the same.

CHAPTER 16

Two of a Kind

THE CURATOR WAS not at all like Megan expected. She remembered the curator at the local museum, a tired, worn-looking man in a flecked, gray business suit that matched the salt and pepper colour of his thin, receding hair. This curator was young and wore a high-crowned black felt western hat, a plaid shirt, faded blue jeans and pale gray leather riding boots topped with braid. Over the plaid shirt she wore a gray, suede leather vest with tassels at the pockets and waist.

"Where did you say you found it?"

"Outside the tent. A man dropped it."

"And you say your friend saw this man crawl out from under the back of this tent?"

Megan nodded. "And then we saw him arguing with Old Wally, in sign language. We didn't know it was Wally at the time."

"Mm. I'm going to unlock the case and have a look at that buckle."

The curator took a small, silver key from her pocket and inserted it in the brass keyhole. There was a sharp click as she turned the key.

"Excuse me, please." The curator ushered some people back as she lifted the lid and reached into the display case. She held the buckle in her hand as if weighing it. Then she gave to buckle to Megan and locked the showcase once more.

The buckle was very heavy, much heavier than the buckle Megan had found. But it looked exactly the same.

Fifteen minutes later Megan and the curator were in the RCMP tent talking to the duty officer.

This is a fake," said the curator. "It's made of lead. Watch this."

Megan watched as the young woman took a piece of paper and rubbed the edge of the buckle across it; she'd done the same at the Show Tent. A black, wiggly line, like a pencil mark appeared.

"This one, the buckle Megan found, is genuine." She turned it over. "See. It's tarnished on the back where it hasn't been polished, and there's old silver polish in those cracks. Someone made a cast of the real buckle, made a copy in lead, and put the copy in the showcase.

"Why?" Megan couldn't understand why someone would go to all that trouble when they had stolen the buckle anyway.

The curator smiled. "I believe they hoped the theft would go unnoticed for some time. The collection goes to three more locations in the next three weeks."

"But when you pack the buckles to move them, wouldn't you notice?"

"No, Megan. We don't handle them more than is needed. We cover them with a velvet cover and then put Styrofoam, specially made to fit, on top. The buckles won't be cleaned for several months."

"Oh." Now Megan understood. "So, if I hadn't found the buckle you would never have known where or when it was stolen."

"That's right," said the policeman. "And, because the show has come from two other rodeos, there would be six places we'd have to investigate."

"And the museum storage location," said the curator. "A switch could be made there, too."

"Right. Good point." The policeman smiled. "But because of this young lady we can hopefully solve this case quickly." He stroked his moustache. "I have a call in for Paduto and Sanders, they were dealing with this last night." He put on his RCMP Stetson. "In the meantime we must let your parents know you've been found, Megan."

Megan sighed. Now she was for it. "Who told Mum and Dad I was missing?" she said.

The policeman smiled. "I'm not sure anyone *has* told them. We only found out ten minutes back when your friend Samantha got a message to one of our volunteers. She was worried sick, poor kid. It was Samantha who told us your mum and dad are at the rodeo performance." He turned to a volunteer seated at the other desk. "Has Gayle left for the arena, Matt?"

"I'll check." The volunteer picked up a radio receiver.

Megan thought for a moment. "Do we have to tell them right now? Dad's been so looking forward to seeing the rodeo."

The policeman smiled. "You're safe. And what they don't know won't hurt them, is that it?"

Megan nodded.

The radio receiver was crackling. "Control. I'll be at the arena in five minutes."

"Roger." Matt looked over at the RCMP officer.

The policeman pursed his lips and stroked his fair, bristly moustache. "Tell Gayle that Megan is safe with us, and she can return here, Matt." He turned to Megan. "Your folks will have to know eventually," he said.

"I know," said Megan. "But if they find out now Dad won't be able to enjoy the rodeo, and I won't be able to help any more in solving this mystery."

The policeman laughed. "I see. And what do you have in mind?"

"Megan, that really is a great plan." Constable Paduto smiled. "What do you say, Mrs. Perry? Can Megan help? It's our best chance of catching Frank Deeze."

Megan sat anxiously waiting. She had only just learned that Constable Paduto had talked with Old Wally Deeze earlier in the morning. The police officer had found Skipper Tompkins at the bed and breakfast, but hadn't tracked down Old Wally till just before the first rodeo events. At first Wally had denied seeing his brother Frank, but finally he had admitted seeing him outside the Show Tent, as Megan and Samantha had described.

"Why did he lie?" asked Samantha.

"Family, I would think," said Mrs. Liang. "That old saying is true: Blood is thicker than water. His brother is a thief, but he's still his young brother."

Megan saw Samantha nod. If Tony or Jack were in trouble she'd try to protect them, too. But how far did you go?

"That's right," said Constable Sanders. "More often than not it works that way, especially if the brothers or sisters are close. There's less than a year between Frank and Wally; they grew up almost as twins. Wally is obviously upset and tried to protect his brother. Skipper Tompkins told us Wally's been withdrawn and quiet these past two days, keeping to himself and not talking, not signing, that is."

"What's the mystery about Frank?" asked Tony. "Why was he kicked off the circuit?"

"Cheating," said Constable Sanders.

"It was more than cheating." Constable Paduto shook her head, pursing her lips. "He could have killed someone. Skipper Tompkins told us that Frank was a superb saddle-bronc rider but he was so anxious to be a champion, and win this buckle, that he would stop at nothing. He interfered with the equipment of other competitors so they came off the horse. Some were badly injured."

"Did he go to jail?" said Megan.

"No, not enough evidence. But he was shunned and warned off." Constable Paduto sighed. "For a person like Frank that can be worse than jail. But, back to our plan."

"Can I ask a question?"

Megan had been watching Sam's father and had wondered when he'd speak up. He was obviously worried about something.

"Carry on, sir," said Constable Sanders.

"Well, do you think Wally is telling the truth when he says he doesn't know where his brother is? If he's lying the girls could be in danger."

The police officers exchanged glances. Constable Paduto spoke: "I don't think he does know, Mr. Liang. He says he told Frank that if he saw him again he'd tell all the rodeo folk. And my guess is he has no idea Frank is using the clown disguise in his efforts to regain the buckle."

"Right." Constable Sanders nodded. "And after Wally lied to officer Paduto about not having seen Frank she wasn't going to tell him about the clown disguise."

"So, are you saying that the girls won't be in any danger?"

"We'll have people watching them at all times, Mrs. Perry." Constable Sanders nodded. "And the Lone Star barn will be staked out."

Megan looked at Mum. She had to agree! If she agreed to the plan Megan knew they'd catch Frank, because now they knew his tricks: First he'd worn a clown disguise like Roly Poly Fred; then an outfit like DeeDee; and the green outfit she'd seen him wearing earlier was like Shamrock Pete's. The next time he'd probably be dressed like Corky in a hobo outfit, with patched jeans, an old tweed jacket and bright orange tie, and a floppy white sun hat. But the face would be the same and everyone looking for him would have a photocopy of her drawing.

Mum and Dad were now talking quietly, almost whispering. Megan couldn't hear a word. Mum said it was rude to whisper. They went over to Sam's parents. They talked quietly, first nodding, then shaking their heads, and then nodding again. But as Dad came over she knew they'd reached a decision.

"We'll go along with it as long as Jack and Tony can be with them."

Mr. and Mrs. Liang were nodding.

"Sounds like a good idea to me, Mr. Perry." Constable Sanders looked over at his partner. "Any problems, Joan?"

"No problems." Constable Paduto shook her head. "Let's get the show on the road." She smiled. "We'll raid the Lone Star Enterprises barn when we have Frank Deeze safely in custody."

CHAPTER 17

Billy Butts In

"TELL ME AGAIN why the petting zoo will be closed, Meg." Jack's voice croaked when he said zoo.

Megan looked at her brother. That was the problem with Jack, why he was always in trouble; he didn't listen. But now he was beet-red, looking at Samantha.

"Didn't you listen, Jack?"

Jack looked sideways, not looking up. "I was listening, but I was also listening to the messages on the police radio. "His voice croaked again. Jack scowled.

Megan sighed. She couldn't help it if Jack was embarrassed, this was too important.

"The zoo tent will be closed because they don't want anyone there." She went on quickly. "Now, if Frank Deeze follows Sam and me, sees us go into the tent while there's a big CLOSED sign up, he might follow us in."

"Oh, yes." Jack nodded. "I'd forgotten."

"Well," said Tony, "Jack and I won't let you guys out of sight. We'll be behind you."

Megan smiled. She felt safe, knowing her brothers would be close by. The police had changed her plan. Jack and Tony wouldn't walk with them, as Deeze might not try to steal the buckle if he saw four of them together, but he would probably act if he saw just the two girls. She turned the fake buckle over and over in her hand. It would be fun to catch the thief at his own game.

"We'd better split up now."

"Okay, Meg, I can see one of the undercover men in place. Good luck. And you, Sam."

"Thanks, Tony." Megan started to walk slowly up the path leading to the booths. She put the fake buckle in her pocket and smiled at Sam "Are you nervous?"

Samantha nodded. "A little bit, Meg. But with Jack and Tony and the undercover people keeping watch I don't see what can go wrong." She grinned. "Anyway, all this excitement has made me really hungry."

Megan smiled. She was hungry, too. The plan was to stop at the Wranglers Barbecue and get a Wranglers Whopper. While they ate the Wranglers hamburger Megan would pretend to show Samantha the fake buckle. The police thought that if Deeze himself wasn't in the crowd nearby there would probably be one or more of the young gang that had attacked the girls; they'd recognize the girls and report to Deeze.

"I can almost taste the hamburger," said Megan, "I'm so hungry. And I think I'll get a milkshake."

"That would be too much for me," said Sam. "I'll just have a small cream soda. It's great being able to get those here, I haven't had one since we left South Africa."

The delicious smells coming from the food stalls made Megan want to run to Wranglers. But if they did that they might lose the boys and the undercover people. She concentrated on walking as slowly as possible.

There was no sign of Frank Deeze. She thought she'd seen one of the girls in the gang, but when she tried to point her out to Samantha the girl was gone. At last they reached the hamburger stand.

"Two whoppers, please." Megan looked at the woman behind the counter.

"All the makings, love?"

"Yes please," said Meg.

"No onions, thank you," said Sam. "They give me indigestion."

"Okay, love." The woman turned to a man at the grill. "Two Wranglers special Whoppers, one no onions," she shouted.

Megan wondered why she had to shout.

"He's half-deaf," said the woman. "Anything else?"

"I'll have a special milkshake," said Megan. She looked over at the grill where two large beef patties were now sizzling. They looked great.

"What flavour, love?"

Megan wondered whether to have pineapple or Banana. "Pineapple, please, and a cream soda for Sam."

"Sam?" The woman looked puzzled.

Samantha laughed. "Me," she said. "Samantha."

The woman laughed. "Ah! Okay. Is that it?"

Megan nodded and reached into her pocket for the money the police had given her. As she pulled her hand out the buckle fell to the ground. She stooped to pick it up and felt that she was being watched. She looked up. There was the girl again, smiling as she turned and walked quickly away.

"That's a real oldie." Said the woman. "Very nice. Can I have a look?"

Megan passed her the buckle. The woman almost dropped it. "A bit heavy, isn't it? I wouldn't want this on my belt."

Megan took the buckle back and returned it to her pocket. This was better than planned. She was sure the girl had seen the buckle. Deeze would get the message soon.

The hamburgers were enormous and they had to find a place to sit down. Megan bit into hers. It really was the best. It wasn't just the taste of the secret recipe barbecue sauce or the toasted bun, it was the whole thing. The meat was juicy, but with no hint of fat and the lettuce and tomato was fresh. She saw Tony and Jack looking at her enviously. She took a slow, deliberate bite.

"Over there." Samantha's voice was barely above a whisper. "By the Taco stand."

Without turning her head, Megan looked over her bun and to the side, pretending to take another bite. There was the bright orange tie. Under the floppy white hat the face had a lopsided look; it was Deeze, it had to be! She finished chewing and then took a sip of her milkshake.

"We'll keep an eye on him, Sam, and finish our meal. Let's see what he does."

"Okay," Sam's reply was muffled as she bit into her bun. "Boy! These hamburgers really are the best, Meg."

Megan nodded. She took another sip from her milkshake and carefully looked towards the clown. He was joking with a small crowd but every once in a while he'd glance her way. She decided that as she'd finished her hamburger she'd pretend to show Sam the buckle. She took it from her pocket. Sun glinted off the silver-coloured metal.

"He's seen it," she whispered, "but he's still joking with those people. He doesn't know it, but one is an undercover police officer." She returned the buckle to her pocket. "Come on. Let's go. We'll see what he does."

"Okay." Samantha drained her drink and stood up. "He's looking this way, Meg."

"Not too fast," said Megan. "We don't want to lose him. Good. The boys are following."

"Are we going to the Petting Zoo?"

"Yes. The sooner he makes a move the better." Megan shivered. "Now it's happening, I just want to get it over and done."

"Me, too. But not so fast, Meg."

Megan slowed down. She must have quickened her pace without realizing it. She stopped and pretended to watch some people throwing darts at balloons.

"Three throws for a dollar!" shouted the man in the booth, holding out three darts with red plastic flights. "Win a lovely prize!"

Megan shook her head and, as she did so, looked sideways. He was there. But where were the boys? Ah. There they were, a little way behind. She walked on.

"We're almost there, Meg."

"I know." Megan felt her stomach tighten. She felt sick. Why had she suggested this? She shrugged. No turning back, now. There was the sign on the tent flap. CLOSED. She unhooked the flap and went inside. The pony whinnied. Billy looked up, blinking. As soon as Samantha was inside Megan let the flap fall, but not before she'd seen the clown staring at the tent. Would he come?

Ten minutes passed. Nothing happened. Megan looked at Sam and shrugged. She felt the buckle heavy in her pocket. She was tempted to open the flap a fraction and look out. She stood by the entrance, wondering if she should. It wouldn't hurt, would it? Carefully she moved a small section of canvas with a forefinger. He wasn't there. The boys were there, but as she watched she saw a gang of youths closing in around them. Oh, no! Instinctively she moved back to the centre of the tent.

Outside the tent voices were raised in anger. They were young voices.

Then, almost a whisper: "Give it to me!" The voice was menacing.

Megan had heard nothing, but there was the clown, one hand over Sam's mouth, the other behind her neck. He must have come in under the canvas at the back of the tent, as he had at the Show Tent. Why hadn't she thought of that? Sam's eyes were wide with fright and Megan saw her flinch, the fright turning to pain, as the man squeezed her neck.

"The buckle! I know you've got it. I saw you at the Wranglers stand." The man pushed Samantha in front of him, his hand still firmly over her mouth. "No tricks and don't think of shouting!"

Megan glanced behind her. The noise and shouting continued outside. Where were the undercover police? They should be here. The man was very close now, his eyes cruel behind the makeup. Megan made up her mind. She reached into her pocket, pulled out the buckle, and held it high over her head.

The clown's eyes changed. He let go Samantha's neck and reached out. But he was too late. Megan threw the buckle into Billy's pen. As she did so she saw Sam squirm free, kicking the man's shins.

"Why, you . . . !" The clown at first tried to grab Samantha, but then he seemed to change his mind, bounding forward over the fence. Billy took a step back and then, as the clown bent to recover the buckle, he charged, his head down.

"Yow!" The man fell to the ground and, as he scrambled to get up, searching in the straw for the buckle, Billy put his head down again. Wham! Deeze was ready this time and sidestepped neatly. Billy hit the fence and turned, shaking his head. The clown had found the buckle and, as Billy got ready to charge again, he vaulted the fence.

But Megan had anticipated that. The man was very agile. She had opened the gate and Billy saw his chance. He bounded after the clown and caught him as he bent to lift the canvas at the back of the tent. This time Billy hit him squarely. The clown got up, limping.

But Billy wasn't finished. Now that he was loose it was as if he was in the rodeo arena. Billy charged. The clown sidestepped. Billy charged again. The man jumped into an empty feed bin, his floppy white hat flying off as he ducked down inside. Megan watched. What was happening? If she didn't know differently she would swear this was Old Wally.

CHAPTER 18

A Grand Finale

"YOU WERE RIGHT, Megan." Constable Paduto smiled. "Yesterday, when we raided the Lone Star Enterprises barn we found Old Wally. At first we didn't find him. The place was so full of stolen items it was like a supermarket: stolen goods with price tickets stacked up row upon row."

"Price tickets?" said Megan.

"Oh, yes." The police officer smiled. "The word would have been sent round in two or three weeks from now. Some people, more than a few, don't care that they're buying 'hot' or stolen goods. They would have come to shop for things they wanted: stereos, CB radios, iPods, CD players, Walkmans . . ."

"CD players!" Jack jumped up. "Did you find my CD player?"

"I expect we will, Jack," said Constable Paduto. "We'll have a look later today. The CD section isn't that large, but there are hundreds of other items, if not thousands. It will take days to take inventory and check it all with our reports. Anyway, it wasn't until we looked in a small room at the back that we found Old Wally. He was bound and gagged."

"Was he hurt?" asked Tony.

Constable Sanders shook his head. "Not really. Old Wally's tough." He smiled. "And so he should be after all the rodeo injuries he's recovered from."

Megan had been listening, thinking. "What I don't get," she said, "is how Frank fooled everyone for two days like that?"

"I wondered about that, too," said Samantha.

Megan looked sideways at her friend. Sam had been really brave. Angry red finger marks stood out on her neck. Sam had a sort of whiplash and her neck was very painful. Megan shivered. She still didn't like to think of the mean look in Frank Deeze's eyes when he held Sam yesterday.

"Well, remember that Frank was on the major rodeo circuit for many years before he was black-listed," said Constable Sanders. "Rodeo life is in his blood. For a while, after he was shunned, he made the rounds of the minor shows. With grease paint to disguise his face no one recognized him. He became a clown."

"So that's how he knew the basic moves," said Tony. "When I got the rubbing of Old Wally's buckle, the cowboy who helped me with sign language, so I could talk to Wally, said bulls have difficulty turning in small circles, so the clowns stay close to them and keep turning."

"Mm. I didn't know that," said Constable Sanders.

"It didn't help Frank Deeze with Billy," said Megan. "Old Billy butted him the first time and then kept on butting him into the canvas at the back of the zoo tent until the undercover police got there."

"That's true. Our Billy should be given a medal. It's not the first time he's cornered a thief." Mum smiled.

Megan stared at Mum and then sighed with relief. She hadn't seen Mum smile since she and Dad and the Liangs had been called to the RCMP tent last night. Perhaps things would settle down now. Megan smiled.

"Anyway," continued the policeman, "there isn't much money to be made on the minor circuits, so Deeze turned to theft. The grease paint became even more useful now. He could be seen but not seen."

"And even though he took a new name," added Constable Paduto, "he really kept his own."

"How?" said Tony. "How could he change his name and keep it?"

Constable Paduto smiled. "He took the letters of his own name and mixed them up. He called himself Derek Fanze."

"That was clever," said Jack. "But I still don't see how he fooled everyone. He would know how to sign because Wally had been handicapped from birth. But how did he know Wally's act, what to do in the arena?"

"Do you remember last night?" asked Constable Sanders. "When Samantha's mum said that blood is thicker than water?"

Jack nodded.

"Well, when Frank ventured onto the major circuit again, and started to organize his theft ring, he would watch his brother. He couldn't resist. He came to know the moves, and he told us that he'd really enjoyed himself these last two days. He was in the rodeo again, in the arena, with crowds shouting and clapping for him. The only thing that spoiled it was losing the buckle for a second time."

"A second time?" said Megan. "Was it his?"

"No. Not really." Constable Sanders shook his head. "What I mean, Megan, is that the year he was caught cheating he was one of the top riders. He believed he'd win and so did everyone else. But he wanted to be certain. He cheated, was caught and lost his chance at the buckle."

Megan sighed. First he'd tried to steal it by cheating. Now he'd stolen it for real and would go to jail. And what about the kids he'd involved?

"Will the kids go to jail, too?"

"No. They'll be dealt with, of course, but I'll have to explain that another time. Constable Paduto smiled. "Now, the reason we asked you all to be here this afternoon is to tell you how the investigation has proceeded so far, and to thank you." She held up her hand. "No talking, please. And . . ." she looked over at the entrance to the tent.

Megan saw the Show Tent curator. She wore the same high crowned, black felt hat, but it now had an Indian beadwork band. And her tasseled vest was covered in matching, intricate beadwork. Today she wore black boots with silver spurs, and black jeans. She stood aside and the mayor came in, a big smile on his face.

"So," said Constable Paduto. "I'll ask the mayor to explain."

The final rodeo performance was over and the presentations about to begin. Megan heard the voice of the announcer over the speakers.

"Well, folks," he drawled. "This has been a real good show today, good clean fun, none of that false TV violence and in-your-face advertising. All the competitors have been great and we've had no serious injuries. We can give thanks for that." He paused. "And Old Wally outdid himself. He was almost as good as that old rooster pulling him around in that barrel."

There were roars of laughter.

"But, folks, today I want to tell you about Megan, Samantha, Tony and Jack . . ." there was a pause and the speakers crackled. The voice came faintly through. "A goat? Oh, right." Now the voice resumed. "As I said: Megan, Samantha, Tony, Jack and Billy-the-goat. Would you young folk step into the arena, please? And Billy, of course."

Megan felt more nervous than at any time over the weekend, even when Frank Deeze had suddenly appeared in the Petting Zoo. The curator, whose name she now knew was Lisa, smiled as she stood up. Lisa was nice. She'd allowed Tony to take rubbings of all the Vintage Collection buckles. She led the way through the reserved section of the stands. Megan felt embarrassed with all the people looking at her. Why did they do that?

The arena had been raked, but in the late afternoon sun the smell of sawdust and wood chips and animals was still strong. Megan heard people clapping and realized that in her shyness she had shut out the voice of the announcer.

"And now, folks, the mayor will present the buckles. Megan."

"I can't believe it," said Tony, later that evening as he followed Megan up the stairs of the old farmhouse.

Megan smiled. Tony had been bursting with excitement all evening. He had the rubbings of the Vintage Collection; rubbings of the buckles of most of the champions at the rodeo this year; and he had Old Wally's, of course and, a rubbing of Frank's buckle. Old Wally had visited his brother in the police cells and Frank had agreed to let Tony copy his buckle; he'd said that if someone was that keen on rodeo he couldn't refuse. The buckle had a big D in the centre like Wally's, but crossed by a small, lower case 'f' and not a 'w' like Walley's.

"This has been just the greatest weekend, Meg."

"I know." Megan felt so good that she wanted to shout. "And when Mum and Dad said we weren't going to move, because if they did we wouldn't be able to keep Billy, that was the best news."

Tony nodded. "I don't know what I'd have done without that old beast." He smiled. "Dad's going to start on Mum's office next week. Isn't that great?"

Megan nodded. Things had worked out after all. But, she wondered if they'd be in the bed race next year. She yawned.

"Goodnight, Tony. See you in the morning."

CPSIA information can be obtained at www.ICGtesting.com
Printed in the USA
LVOW051243131212

311376LV00001B/31/P